for with Nicola.

The Case of the Barking Dog

A Callum Lange Mystery

Nicola Pearson

This story is a work of fiction.
No part of the contents relate to any real person or persons, living or dead.

Copyright © 2013 Nicola Pearson

ISBN-13: 978-1499574593
ISBN-10: 1499574592

Acknowledgements

I learned, when I started to write this mystery, that I really knew very little about crime scenes so my first thanks go out to Detective Theresa Luvera of the Skagit County Sheriff's Office for setting me straight on the facts. Thanks also to Pat Buller for plant specifics, Kiawa Warford for help with the setting and Jerry Ziegler for his editorial feedback and constant encouragement. Jason Miller, editor and publisher of the Concrete Herald, gets a big shout out for agreeing to publish this mystery in serial format and, as a result, thanks also to Davey Silverman and Mary Ann Wisman for always letting me know just how *much* they were looking forward to the next installment. Finally thanks to my husband, Stephen Murray, and our children, who continually read and support my work. You make it all worthwhile.

Cover Art:

Original photograph of Sauk Mountain taken by Chuck Bussiere. Graphic design by Jon-Paul Verfaillie.

For Liz,
who said the right words in the right order for
Callum Lange to pop into my head.

It was the sound of the emergency vehicles screaming along the highway some hundred and fifty feet below that woke Lange. The first sped into his subconscious and became part of his dream, the second snapped his head upright and the third set his teeth on edge. Or maybe it was the large scotch he'd drunk before nodding off at the computer that was responsible for the metallic taste in his mouth. Damn, he hated falling asleep at the computer.

Lange blinked blearily and rolled his head from side to side on his shoulders, trying to get the crick out of his neck. He touched the space bar on his laptop, to see what time it was, and the screen lit up, garishly presenting him with an empty document page, the cursor still blinking in the top left corner. He smacked his tongue against the roof of his mouth then glanced at the time; 6:30 a.m.. It had been a very short night.

But then it was the night of July 4th and everybody in the Upper Skagit had been setting off fireworks it seemed like. Lange thought he'd get to avoid all that, living way up on Sauk Mountain, and had sat down at his computer to work on a story when the explosions began, interrupting his thoughts enough times that he'd finally yielded to the celebration, poured himself a glass of Chivas Regal and gone and sat on his log pile outside. At least out there it was cooler than it was inside his yurt and he could see the lights and color that went with the noise of the fireworks. He'd nestled his buttocks into a partial piece of vinyl-covered, foam pad that he'd found at the dump and leaned his back against the smaller diameter logs heaped on top of the pile. He always felt like King of the Mountain sitting on his log pile, looking down at the valley below. From this vantage point he could see the great Skagit River snaking silver and blue through the lush landscape of the valley around it. He could see intermittent flashes of the highway and the occasional homestead. He could see the trees on the mountain ridges opposite changing color as the shade of the day moved with the clouds. But most importantly, he could see billows of pink and lavender, sometimes red, gold, fuchsia, mauve, airbrushing a visual symphony in the sky as the sun rose and set in his mountain dell.

Last night he'd sat watching artificial bursts of glitter and flame shooting through the valley until their supply had been exhausted. Then he'd sipped his scotch, while the chain of dogs, led by one that was obviously spooked by the fireworks, slowly quieted down their barking until there was nothing but peace. A peace like nowhere else in the world, sitting on the side of Sauk, punctuated only by the gentle swishing of the boughs of the cedar trees around him as the breeze moved through them. Lange sat until he'd absorbed his fill and was about to go back inside when a pair of owls broke the silence, hooting their interest in each other through the trees. He was instantly mesmerized by the clarity of their call and couldn't bring himself to move in case he interrupted their wooing. Their woo-hooing.

It must have been 2 a.m. before the rain clouds drifted in from the west, making their entrance so discreetly that first a few stars disappeared, then the moonlit mountain ridges opposite and finally Lange could smell the moisture in the air around him and knew he'd been cloaked. That's when he dragged himself off the logs and made his way back to the computer, hoping to write his story. Apparently he'd fallen asleep as soon as he landed in his chair.

Oh well, there was always today, he told himself as he stretched to a stand and started the short shuffle across the yurt to his bed. The place was a mess, with games and puzzles on overturned milk crates scattered around the plywood floor and dirty mugs, bowls and plates sitting beside them. It was just as well Suleka was coming with his groceries today. She was always good for sprucing up the yurt when he let it get too out of hand.

Before Lange got to his bed a fourth emergency vehicle wailed through the canvas walls and stopped him in his tracks. Why would they need a fourth vehicle? Usually an accident up in the Pass required an ambulance and a State Patrol car – sometimes two – but rarely did he hear four vehicles go sailing by. He was telling himself to ignore it, that maybe it was a wreck that needed more than one ambulance, when a fifth and then a sixth set of tires went thundering over the blacktop, sirens screeching at full peal.

His curiosity piqued and his mind now fully awake, Lange picked up a pair of binoculars he had lying next to his bed and took a couple of steps to the right, to look out the window that was directly opposite the door in the circle of his yurt. But before he could position the binoculars inside the wooden lattice that ran between the sheets of plastic forming the window, the seventh emergency vehicle sped by. Now Lange moved fast, springing easily over three piles of hunting and fishing magazines as he dashed across the yurt, avoiding his desk in the center, and tugged open the door. For a 60-year-old man he was still lean and muscular, maybe even more than when he'd been working in New York because out here, he spent a lot of time hiking up and down Sauk Mountain Road and chopping firewood. The only thing that gave away his retirement was the length of his thick, white hair. He pushed it out of his eyes as he crossed the short deck on the other side of the door. There was garbage strewn all over the ground at the bottom of the steps. Damn, that raccoon must have been back after he'd gone to sleep last night! Maybe he'd talk Suleka into cleaning that up too. He went down the two steps and swiftly picked his way past the garbage, being careful not to step on any of it with his bare feet. Then he darted through the grassy ground cover, still wet from the overnight rain, and made his way to the edge of the ridge. He'd heard two more sets of sirens as he was moving, along with the distant echoes of a barking dog, and he trained his binoculars east, down the highway, to see where they might be going. The vehicles weren't hard to follow, their lights spinning like beacons, and Lange watched them continue straight for a couple of miles then turn right and speed over the narrow bridge crossing the Skagit River in Rockport. Then they spun left, onto the Harmony Ranch Road, followed it around to the right and disappeared in a thicket of trees. Lange thought for a moment then climbed up onto his log pile and cautiously edged his way along to the far end. He raised up the binoculars and saw red and blue twinklings through the copse of trees. That must be the site of the incident,

Lange sighed. He'd moved to the Upper Skagit after retiring because he'd never forgotten the two heavenly summers he'd spent here as a boy, staying at his Uncle Glen's house in Concrete. Uncle Glen died before Lange graduated high school but he'd subscribed to the Concrete Herald for his nephew and Lange had maintained the subscription. And the worst thing he'd ever read in the sheriff's blotter was the case of a woman calling the cops to say she'd woken up to find a strange man in her bed. The sheriff had investigated and found that the woman had been seen leaving the local tavern with the man the previous night so the sheriff closed the case by warning the woman of the dangers of casual sex. After thirty years of dealing with senseless, bloody murders in NYC, Lange had jumped at the chance to buy 80 acres on Sauk and spend the rest of his years looking at a crimeless paradise.

Flashing lights with no sirens drew Lange's attention back down to the highway. He peered through his binoculars. There it was; the dark green of the coroner's van. Suddenly Lange felt like a deer sensing a predator. His head lifted, his stomach tightened and his ears began to twitch. He'd never felt this living in New York, probably because he was around so many predators in that city he'd become immune to the signals. But standing here, on the side of Sauk, Lange's predator response made itself instantly known. And as his ears flexed back and the hairs at the nape of his neck stood up, Lange got the impression that the predator he was feeling was somewhere on the mountain behind him.

*****

"Callum, are you up?"

It was the second rude awakening for Lange that morning. This time, though, he was lying in his bed and when his eyes opened despite himself he found himself staring up at the pinnacled dome of his yurt wondering what was going on. He brought his eyes back down and could see Suleka through the glass in the top half of the door, awkwardly looking down at her feet.

"I've got your groceries and I'll bring them in only I don't want to find you in there naked or something."

Lange sucked in a loud breath and swung his legs over the side of the bed. "I'm up and I'm dressed," he reassured Suleka. He wasn't dressed exactly but he was decent in his sweatpants and t-shirt. And hot, from falling back to sleep with the sun streaming through the skylight in the peak of the canvas roof.

"You know you oughta put something on top of your garbage can to stop the raccoons from getting into it," Suleka said, keeping her eyes on the outside as she backed into the yurt carrying two bags of groceries. "Something heavy that they can't move off. 'Course, that won't work if it's a bear...."

"What time is it?" Lange asked.

"I don't know. Maybe 10:15."

"You're late."

Suleka spun around to face Lange, her thick, dark brown braid with its silver highlights swinging off her shoulder to hang down her back in the process. She wasn't a handsome woman with her long jaw, close-set hazel eyes and thickening waistline but she had a heart of gold and at 63 she was done taking backtalk. "Like you're on a deadline, still in bed at this time of the morning!"

Lange sat up to his full height. "I worked late last night."

"Oh right. On your stories. How far d'you get this time?" She glanced at the laptop open on the desk under the skylight as she took a few steps to the left and set the bags of groceries on a length of Formica counter-top next to the kitchen sink.

Lange, catching her glance, rose and crossed to his laptop. "I'm still on the first page," he grunted and closed the lid so she couldn't see exactly where on the first page. He went around his desk and joined her next to the sink, watching as she unpacked his groceries.

"Why do you want to write hunting and fishing stories?" Suleka asked, transferring apples and bananas to a wooden bowl on the counter top. "Why don't you pick something you know to write about?"

"I know about hunting and fishing! I've been out many times after deer...."

"But you've never killed one."

"Well no," Lange agreed. He followed a 2 x 4 board from the sidewall of the yurt up to the skylight with his eyes. "I don't want to deal with the blood."

Suleka puckered her lips cynically. "I bet that'll make riveting reading."

Lange ignored the comment, allowing her to move past him to the refrigerator with some milk and eggs. "Why were you late?"

"None of your business!"

Lange peered out the window opposite, at all the shades of green he could see through the plastic, and waited for her to give the reason.

"My husband walked out on me last night," she admitted finally. Then she turned and looked over the top of her glasses at Lange, expecting some snarky remark. She was grateful when he didn't give one. "It wasn't what I was expecting at my advanced years." She paused, trying to contain her emotions before walking past him back to the bags of groceries. "Between that and some dog in the neighborhood that wouldn't stop barking after about 3 a.m., I had a rough night."

Lange watched her pull two cans of soup out of one of the bags and stash them under the counter on a shelf. "I don't like that brand," he complained. "Too much salt."

"You want to be picky, you can do your own shopping."

"You know I don't drive."

Suleka pounced. "Then why keep a Prius parked at the bottom of Sauk Mountain Road?"

"In case I ever *have* to drive."

She fixed him with a stare then began shelving beans, cereal and cookies. "You know people think you're weird."

"That's okay. I think people are weird."

He pushed himself away from the counter-top he was leaning against and walked around his desk to stand by the window. He focused on the place in the distance where he'd seen the lights twinkling through the trees earlier. "I thought you were late because of whatever was going on this morning on the Harmony Ranch Road."

"I wondered how long it would take you to ask me about that."

"I wasn't asking…."

"Sure you were…."

Lange sniffed a big lungful of air. A part of him thought he was better off not knowing what had gone down in the pastoral peace of Rockport so early in the morning but another part of him was furious that someone had thought to contaminate that peace with crime. And whatever they'd done, he didn't want them getting away with it. "Okay I was," he admitted.

Suleka put a package of grass-fed, beef tenderloin steaks in the fridge as she put him out of his misery. "A young woman was found stabbed to death in her home up there. Dinah Haddock. You know her?"

Lange shook his head no. He would have remembered a name like Haddock.

"Well you didn't miss much," Suleka said, again with that cynical pucker to her lips. Lange was surprised. Suleka was gruff and sassy but he'd never heard her speak ill of anyone before. He moved towards her and leaned against the counter again as she opened a bag of ground coffee and poured the contents into a hand-made, pottery jar. "She was definitely not a pleasant person," she added.

"In what way?"

"She was hostile and petty and passive aggressive. And good at winding people up, making them want to…..." Her hand tightened on the bag of coffee. "……do bad things to her."

"She made you feel like that?"

"Several times," Suleka admitted. Then her head shot up and she spilled some coffee on the counter as the implication of what she'd just said came to her. She glared at Lange. "Hey, I was at home last night, being dumped by my husband!"

"I wasn't accusing you…."

"Sure you were. You're a detective. That's what you do."

"An ex-detective," Lange corrected and shifted the fruit bowl so she could scoop up the spilled coffee. "Who found her?"

"A co-worker. From the Park Service." Suleka tipped what she'd retrieved of the ground coffee into the jar, brushed her hands off over the sink and wiped the counter with a dishrag. "I guess she stopped by this morning to pick up Dinah to go hiking and when Dinah didn't come to the door, this gal walked into the house and bingo, there was Dinah. Dead on the floor."

"Haddock lived alone?"

"No, she was married."

"So where was the husband?"

"Nobody knows. At least," Suleka went on, as she folded the environmentally friendly, reusable grocery bags flat. "Nobody knew in the post office this morning where I picked up the news."

Lange had been chewing absently on one of the bananas but this latest made him stop and look directly at Suleka. "You didn't go to the crime scene?"

"Why would I?"

"How else will I know what it looks like?"

Suleka fixed him with another stare. She wanted to tell him he should go himself if he wanted to know so much but she knew that would be a waste of time. Callum Lange didn't go anywhere he didn't absolutely have to and then he'd only go if he could walk. She put the folded grocery bags into the top pocket of her denim dungarees. "Do you want me go before or after I clean up the mess you've made of this yurt?"

"Before," Lange ordered. He tossed the empty banana peel into the kitchen sink and moved with renewed energy towards his desk. He opened a drawer and pulled out a smart phone. "Take this with you for photos. I'll walk to the gate where I get a signal, and you can send them to me. If I need close ups, I'll text you."

Suleka looked down at the phone he was handing her. "Isn't this your phone?"

"No, that's a spare." He hurried across the yurt to a chair next to his bed and retrieved a towel. He'd clean himself up outside, under his solar shower, before heading to the gate.

Suleka was still staring down at the cell phone. "Why would you have a second cell phone?"

"For the same reason I have a Prius parked at the bottom of Sauk Mountain Road. In case I ever need it." He moved towards her again and snatched up the bar of soap sitting beside the sink. "You'd better hurry, before those sheriff deputies trample the evidence with their big boots."

Suleka nodded and moved towards the door, all the time asking herself why she would help Lange with this. She'd agreed to shop for his groceries and ferry him around when he needed to leave the property but nothing had ever been said about detective work. And yet here she was, going through the motions as if inclined to help. Maybe she was sensitive to his need to be a part of this investigation. Or maybe she knew that with him on board, there was a chance the local sheriff would catch this killer. And Suleka, like Lange, wanted whoever did this caught.

She walked out the door with Lange close behind. "Oh and Suleka," he said, as he stopped to slip on a pair of sandals.

"Yes?"

"I'm sorry." She furrowed her brow in confusion. "About your husband leaving you."

Now she felt very inclined to help.

****

Lange paced in front of the gate to his property, holding his cell phone in various positions, hoping to catch the messages from Suleka. The phone showed he had service but not much; maybe it took more than one bar to receive photographs. He swatted at the bugs zipping out from the shade of the trees and dive bombing his face and neck, then tried to look invisible as a car bumped past him, swirling clouds of dust from the gravel road like a bridal train behind it. No doubt someone on their way up to hike Sauk Mountain. He looked at his phone once more; still nothing.

He couldn't wait any longer. It had been almost an hour since Suleka took off for the crime scene and Lange needed to know what she'd seen. He began the steep descent down Sauk Mountain Road, glad that he'd changed into ultra lightweight pants and a loose cotton shirt after his outdoor shower. Last night's rain burst certainly hadn't done anything to abate the heat.

He dropped his smart phone into his shirt pocket as his stride gained rhythm and length and almost immediately his mind slipped into the log cabin he planned to build for himself on his property. It would be on the ledge where his log pile was now with a wide porch and glass sliding doors in the front, to capture the view. The downstairs would be one big room with a wood stove someplace central. A wood stove with a glass door, so he could see the flames, and enough space on top to cook a pot of something in the winter.

He was distracted from his thoughts by a sprawling length of tanglefoot berries growing on the upper bank of the road. He stopped, thought about it for a second, then reached his right foot up and anchored it in the base of a tree. He pushed off that to climb the bank, clambering four more steps up through the loose, dry, brushy soil to the berries. He stopped with his feet against a rock and his belly leaning into the shrubs, to sample the tiny fruit. Their sweet, tangy flavor burst on his tongue and he was reminded, once again, of Uncle Glen, who taught him where to look for these berries and when to pick them. Uncle Glen took a great interest in the plant life of the Pacific Northwest and Lange had inherited his books on the subject, as well as his interest, after Glen died. He'd be proud of how much his nephew had learned if they were to meet now, Lange thought, as he popped another wild blackberry in his mouth.

A Ford Expedition crunched over the gravel road below Lange and he looked down in time to catch the gold insignia painted across the dark grey of the outside. The sheriff. Where was he off to, Lange wondered?

He climbed back down, chuckling at the thought that the driver probably hadn't even seen him, and brushed the dust off his pants. They'd had a long, dry spell in the Upper Skagit, despite last night's rain, and this south face of Sauk certainly evidenced that fact. They'd been lucky the July 4th festivities hadn't started any brush fires.

Lange walked another 400 feet downhill and then rounded a bend in the road to find a shady length of undulating gravel road that ran between the trees of the State Park. In the distance, sunlight hit the asphalt on Hwy 20. A skittering in the undergrowth to his left made Lange turn and suddenly a young coyote with a beautiful pelt of grey and gold sprang out of the trees ahead of him. The coyote flicked his head to the right, momentarily bracing Lange with both eyes, then ran even faster into the trees on the other side of the road and was gone. Lange took a half a dozen steps with his eyes to the left, hoping to see whatever had spooked the pup out of the trees at this time of day but when nothing revealed itself, he faced forward and chuckled again, this time at the thought that the coyote *hadn't* missed seeing him.

Lange reached the bottom and began pacing once more, Backwards and forwards across the mouth of Sauk Mountain Road, constantly looking up Hwy 20 towards Rockport, hoping to glimpse Suleka's green Nissan pick-up truck. He had his cell phone in his hand again; it showed 2 bars of service but no texts. Lange grumbled under his breath; what was keeping her? His pacing turned into a determined march towards where he had his Prius parked. He may as well go check on it. But before he turned left into the driveway to the Park Ranger's house, where he'd been allowed to keep his Prius, he saw the Nissan coming down the road towards him. He took two steps back towards the edge of the hard shoulder and signaled Suleka with a nod of his head. Suleka looked surprised but slowed the Nissan to a stop alongside Lange in the middle of the westbound lane of the highway. "What are you doing down here?" she questioned through the open passenger window.

"Where are the photos?" he barked, ignoring her question.

"They wouldn't let me go inside the house so I couldn't take any photos," Suleka replied, glancing in her rear view mirror to make sure no one was coming up behind her. "I nearly had one of the EMTs talked into letting me take a look but then a detective from down valley showed up and said no way."

"Which detective?"

"Frankie Deller."

"She's heading this investigation?"

Suleka shrugged. "I guess."

Lange squinted back up the road, towards Rockport. Francesca. She was good. Probably the only detective he respected in the County Sheriff's office. Her first collar ever she'd pulled over a vehicle for a traffic violation and spotted a gun stuffed down between the front seats when she'd walked up on the driver. Deller had just been listening to an alert on her car radio about a bank robbery not 2 miles from where she'd pulled the vehicle over so she made the driver get out and open the trunk. Sure enough there was the loot. She drew her weapon and made the perp lay down on the ground with his hands behind his head. "You'd better not move," she advised him. "This is my first time."

Lange knew Deller would have no patience with anyone contaminating the crime scene although he suspected she may have arrived too late to ensure that wouldn't be the case. He could use that as an argument for getting a look; his trained eye knew how to look past boot prints in the blood.

"Any word on the husband?" he asked, focusing on Suleka once more.

She nodded her head up and down with her eyes on the rear view mirror again. "Hop in," she ordered, "before this vehicle catches up to me."

Lange followed her directive as a large RV bore down on them. Suleka drove 200 feet forward and jerked her Nissan off the highway at the end of Sauk Mountain Road, put it into park once more and turned to face Lange. "The husband's camped up at Sauk Lake," she explained. "Apparently he hiked in early yesterday and planned to spend two nights, meaning he'd hike out tomorrow. One of the deputies just drove up there to bring him back early. I'm surprised you didn't pass him on the road."

"The husband and wife didn't go camping together," Lange muttered, his brain already trying to form a picture of the dead woman's relationships.

"Maybe they didn't share the same days off," Suleka offered. "That happens with people that work for the Park."

Lange's blue eyes narrowed as he pictured the fireworks zinging in the sky over the Skagit last night. He thought about Dinah, alone at her house, while her husband was alone at Sauk Lake. But then that was an assumption to think that they were both alone. And if 30 years of being on the police force had taught him anything, it had certainly taught him never to assume.

Suleka decided Callum was lost in one of his reveries and she may as well take him home as sit around at the side of the highway. She shifted into drive and turned the steering wheel to the right, to head up the mountain.

"Where are you going?' Lange asked.

"I'm taking you back up to your place. Why? Do you want to walk?"

"No, no, take me over to the crime scene. I'd like to be there when they bring the husband back down."

"Why? It wasn't him."

"Doesn't mean he wasn't involved."

Suleka nodded to herself as she turned the wheels of the truck back towards the highway. "They're looking at the neighbor, you know."

Lange's head whipped in her direction. "Tell me."

"They've been fighting ever since Dinah moved onto that property," Suleka began as she pulled out onto the highway. "Well, he was fighting. She, of course, just maintained her high-handed act of being right and not wanting to discuss it and calling the cops on him at every opportunity. Made him want to slap her, I'm sure."

"What was it about? The fight?"

"Usual up-valley stuff. Something about the property line."

"She thought he was encroaching on her property?"

"She was sure of it. Even though it had never been an issue before she bought the property. But she had the mind of a gnat, the way she honed in on every little opening. And things had to be just the way she wanted them."

"Are they questioning this neighbor?"

"I heard Deller give the instruction."

Lange sucked on the bridge holding his two false teeth in place, then added, "You'd better step on it then. I don't want to miss out on any more."

Ignoring his instruction, Suleka braked as she rounded the corner at the Rockport Store. "Hear that barking?" she asked, pointing out her window to the left.

"Mmm hmmm," Lange replied.

"That's the dog that kept me up half the night. You'd think he'd be past whatever provoked him by now."

But Lange was already wondering if Deller had thought to get a warrant to check the neighbor's knife collection.

*****

The noontime sun beat down on the house in the pasture where the murder had taken place, making the greens of the grass and trees around it seem so vibrant, healthy. If it weren't for the police tape hanging across the front porch this would just be another quaint little cabin in the woods, Lange thought to himself as Suleka stopped the Nissan in the road at the end of the driveway. "You don't have to wait if you don't want to," he told her.

"Good. I didn't intend to," Suleka replied.

"I can walk back from here. Or catch a ride with one of the deputies." Lange swung himself out of the door and turned back to close it. "Do you know the man standing guard at the front door?"

Suleka peeked around Lange's shoulder to see. "That's Alex Osbensky. You know him. He's one of the owners of the grocery store and an EMT with the Rockport Fire Department." Lange gave her a blank look. "Don't you know him?"

Lange glanced back over his shoulder. The portly, unpretentious-looking fellow on the porch waved. Lange looked at Suleka and shrugged, then took off towards the house. He used his piercing blue eyes like a hound dog's nose to hunt for dirt from a shoe, bent blades of grass, maybe a discarded artifact, all the way up the path to the scene of the crime.

"Hi, Callum," Alex greeted him as Lange approached.

"Alex," Lange replied, smiling politely. "I'm here to help, if Detective Deller will allow it," he explained.

The grocery store owner stepped to the right. "She's expecting you," he said, nodding towards the door for Lange to go on in.

Lange didn't hesitate despite being surprised that he was expected. He bounded up the front steps, pushed open the pale wood door – maybe birch, he thought, as his hand grazed the finish – and stepped into the main room of the house. Detective Deller, wearing black dress pants and a white blouse, a .40 caliber Glock in its holster on her right hip, was sideways on to him, bent forward over a couch that was up against the wall to the right. In the background, behind her, hovered a young sheriff's deputy, anxiously waiting to be told to jump. Lange assumed, from the fact that Deller was no longer wearing her white, paper, hazmat suit, that fingerprints and DNA evidence had already been gathered and she was doing her final walk through to make sure nothing had been overlooked. Deller cocked her face in Lange's direction without changing position. "Good. You got my message," she said.

"Message?" he queried, taking in the elegant refinishing of the old homestead cabin. Bamboo flooring, fir trim, smooth, ecru tinted walls. The only disharmonies in the finicky interior were the bloodstains on the floor and furniture around Detective Deller.

"From Officer Collins. Didn't he stop by your place on his way up Sauk?"

"I don't know. I was on my way down by the time he was on his way up and I saw him but I don't think he saw me."

"Figures," tutted Deller, as she straightened to a stand. "So you came out of curiosity?"

"Habit, I'd say. Not one I'm proud of."

Deller gave a small smile. "I'm glad you're here," she told him. Everything about her was businesslike, from the smart clothes and thick braid of dark hair coiled at the back of her head down to the pistol on her hip but Lange found himself drawn to her dark good looks, her svelte figure and her no-nonsense manner. Drawn but not attracted. Apart from anything else she was 25 years his junior. And married.

"Everything intact?" he asked as he circled behind her, examining the splatter patter of the blood.

"Don't get me started!" the detective grumbled, She leaned forward again and, using a pair of tweezers, pulled a tuft of blond hair out of the cushion of the couch.

"That the victim's?" Lange asked, peering over Deller's

shoulder.

She shook her head no. "She was a brunette."

"So what happened, Frankie?" Lange asked, looking down again at the pools of dried blood on the floor.

Frankie Deller bagged the hair and swiveled around to face him. "We're pretty sure Dinah Haddock was asleep on the couch when the killer came in through the door off the utility room in the back, grabbed one of the bar stool cushions in the kitchen and suffocated her with it while – or maybe before – stabbing her repeatedly in the torso."

"A rage killing."

"Seems that way. The cushion was dropped and left at this end of the couch, close by the victim's head and we know where it came from because it was a match to the other one still in the kitchen."

Deller was pointing behind Lange, at the small, high-tech kitchen down a step from the main living area. Lange turned and the young sheriff's deputy moved to the left so Lange would have an unobstructed view of the two bar stools in front of a granite counter, one with a cushion covering the seat, one without. Beyond the deputy, Lange could see an opening that he assumed led to the utility room and the back door.

"And the knife?" he asked, turning to face Deller again.

She shook her head from side to side. "No such luck. We think the cushion was an afterthought. Maybe the killer didn't expect to find her asleep on the couch."

"Time of death?"

"Between midnight and 2 a.m.."

"So the killer probably expected to find her asleep, just not on the couch."

Deller shrugged. It was all conjecture at this point. "It looked like she'd nodded off watching a movie."

"Where's the bedroom?" Lange asked.

Deller turned away from Lange and pointed to a door in the wall opposite, close to the front of the house.

Lange nodded, wondering whether the killer would have used a pillow instead of the cushion if Haddock had been asleep in the bedroom. His eyes moved away from the bedroom door and lingered on the hand-made, wood shelving unit built around the fireplace insert to hold the TV, DVD player and tuner. The wood was strikingly yellow with close set, wavy lines that made it look like a hologram. Curly maple. Beautiful. "And you think she fell asleep watching a movie because…..?"

"The DVD player was still on."

"And the TV."

"No. Not the TV."

"Not the TV," Lange reiterated, nodding his head up and down as if this had significance. "So who turned that off?"

Deller's eyes widened. "Good point. I'll check with the first responders….."

"…because if it wasn't one of them, then it had to be…"

"…the killer." Deller finished, her thoughts synching perfectly with Lange's. "But why would the killer take the time to turn off the TV?"

"Maybe because he likes things orderly," Lange offered, and he let his eyes flick over the detail work in the house once more.

"The husband was camped up at Sauk Lake," Deller stated, knowing where Lange was going with this. She stepped away from the couch, down into the kitchen area and passed the evidence bag of blonde hair to the deputy to take out to the vehicle.

"So I heard," Lange replied. He walked to the end of the couch where Deller had been standing and began studying the surfaces. "But he could have hiked out, driven down, killed his wife and then driven back up and hiked in again."

"I know. And I've got officers on their way to question the kids who were at the top of Sauk, setting off fireworks last night. If nothing else they can corroborate whether his car was at the trailhead between midnight and 2."

"How did you know about the kids with the fireworks?"

"Same way you knew about Haddock's husband being at Sauk Lake. This is a small community."

Lange threw her a withering look. Details. He wanted details.

"One of the first responders said her niece told her about the party at the top of Sauk, wanting to go. She pointed us in the direction of the partiers."

"But you like the neighbor for the murder."

"The neighbor, a number of her co-workers, maybe even the young woman who came to pick her up to go hiking today."

"Why would you go hiking with somebody you hate enough to kill?" Lange asked.

"Habit maybe?" Deller quipped. "And not one she's proud of."

But Lange didn't seem to be listening. He was crouched down, eyes focused on something under the curve of the armrest on the couch. From the intensity of his stare, Deller sensed it was something important.

"What have you found?" she asked, stepping closer to him.

"Seeds."

"On the side of the couch?"

"Sticky seeds. Which is how they got here in the first place."

"Got here when? Last night you think?"

"Possibly," whispered Lange. He half rose, pulled a Swiss Army knife out of the right pocket of his pants and crouched back down, opening the blade.

"You know what they're from?"

Lange didn't answer while he concentrated on lifting some of the tiny seeds off the dark blue upholstery covering the couch. He stood up and held the knife blade out to the light between him and Detective Deller. "I have a suspicion," he replied finally, "although I'd have to check." He lifted his head and met her eyes with his. "But if I'm right, these seeds might just lead us down the path to our killer."

*****

Detective Deller scraped the seeds from Lange's knife into a small paper envelope and walked it down into the kitchen.

"You found Haddock on the floor, I'm guessing," Lange said, as he studied three, amoeba-shaped bloodstains on the cinnamon and brown weave of the bamboo flooring. They were directly between the couch and an overturned coffee table.

"Uh huh," Deller replied. "Face down. That's why we think she may not have been dead when the killer stabbed her. She obviously struggled to get away."

"Feisty," Lange muttered.

"A fighter to the end," agreed Deller.

The young deputy assisting Deller came back into the kitchen via the door from the utility room. "The neighbor just got back home," he told his boss.

"Good. Let's get over there and interview him before he heads out again."

"Can I come?" Lange asked.

"No. You should head up to the Ranger Station in Marblemount and interview Haddock's co-workers. There's one...." She pulled a notebook out of her pants' pocket and looked down at it. "Martin French, that she'd filed a complaint against for sexual harassment. He's worked for the Park for more than 20 years and is apparently well liked. Haddock's complaint was not popular according to the co-worker who found the body." Deller glanced at her notes once more. "Jodie Elliot. Who's a blonde, by the way," she added as she turned on her heels and walked towards the door where the young deputy was still hovering.

Lange didn't move. He sucked on his false teeth thinking about the tuft of blonde hair he'd seen Deller pulling out of the couch. His immobility caused Deller to stop, turn back around, and grace him with a flat look. "Problem?" she asked.

"I wanted to be here when they brought the husband back." Lange admitted.

Deller rolled her eyes. "I sent Deputy Collins after him," she explained. "Do you know Deputy Collins?'

Lange narrowed his eyes as he searched his memory bank. An image formed of a man, 5' 9" maybe, and blocky, with dark, buzz cut hair and an adenoidal way of breathing through his mouth that made him sound like he had a permanent head cold. Lange blinked. "I do. Yes."

"Then you'll know he won't be setting any records hiking to the top of Sauk and down into the lake. What time is it now?"

"12:19," replied Lange, reading the time off the microwave behind Deller's head.

The detective's brown eyes rolled up towards the ceiling as she did a quick, mental computation. "Yeah, I wouldn't expect them back before 5 this evening. Maybe even later. You'll be finished in Marblemount before then."

Lange didn't reply. He was looking at Deller's face but his mind was on the silence of the cabin and its blissful change from the incessant noises of New York. He wanted to stand there longer, savoring that silence, but he knew Deller required an answer. He inhaled sharply, smiled his acknowledgement of what she'd said, then turned away from her to head out. That's when the noises came to him; the girl thrashing from side-to-side, the knife slicing through the air, the blows to the body, the jolts of pain. He wanted to put his hands to his ears, to close them out, but he knew they wouldn't quiet again until he solved the case. Lange walked the short length of the living room feeling aggrieved that this should happen here, in rural Skagit County, when he was suddenly stopped by something. He tilted his head up and to the right. It was his sense of smell, catching a drift on the air that was sweet and pungent. He glanced through the open door to the bedroom. At the end of the bed, sitting on a honey-colored, cedar chest, was a large bouquet of lilacs, the lavender flowers spilling happily in all directions like a head of untamed curls. His spirit lifted at the sight of nature's irrepressibility in the wake of human folly and his step regained a little of its bounce as he walked outside.

Alex Osbensky was still out on the porch doing nothing in particular with a contented half smile on his face. "We've got some asparagus in," he said softly. Lange looked at him, wondering if he was being called on to share gardening stories. "You were asking about it last time you were in the store," Alex added.

Lange's confusion cleared. He loved that the people up here could give of their time for whatever was needed, volunteer fire crew, EMT, ambulance driver, but that didn't stop them from always being in the moment with their real jobs. Maybe if he learned a little of that he'd close down the noises. After all, he wasn't a detective up here, he was a writer. Well he would be once he wrote his first deer-hunting story.

"Thanks," he told Alex with a smile. "I'll have Suleka pick me up some next time she's at your store." He glanced to his right, through the apple trees, to the road that passed in front of the house. "Did you see which way she went when she left?"

"She didn't." Alex nodded at something over to the left of them. "She's at the next driveway along, talking to Too Tall Mo."

Lange spun around to see the bed of Suleka's pick-up truck and the back of a towering beanpole of a man blocking his view of the cab. "Perfect," said Lange. "I'll hitch a ride from her up to Marblemount." He looked at Alex again. "How long are you expected to stand guard over this place?"

"Till Too Tall comes and relieves me," chuckled Alex.

"Want me to nudge him this way?"

"Nah. He'll get here eventually. Then I'll just have to go to work. And I'm kind of enjoying this view of Sauk."

They both turned to the right again. They couldn't see the broad, gnarly top of the local mountain from this angle, just one point at the end of it, along with the expansive cloak of dark green trees that covered the ridge leading up to that point. "And there's only the one trail to the top of Sauk? The one on the south face?" Lange asked.

"Anymore, yes," answered Osbensky. "There's an old, mule trail on the east face that goes all the way from the highway to the top but it hasn't been used in years."

"Where's it come out?"

"Not sure. Up beyond Rockport someplace. Suleka might know."

"Why would she know?"

"Because the trail comes out on a piece of private land that belongs to a Skagit Indian family and she's somehow connected to them. At least, I think she is."

"And you can't access that old trail without crossing the private land?"

"Exactly right."

"Humph," grunted Lange.

With that, he trotted down the steps to the porch and across the grass, passing between two mock orange bushes to access the road. The small, white flowers on the mock orange were in full bloom and Lange felt a catch in his stride as he took a second to imbibe their jasmine-like scent. Then he was once more on the narrow, country road that ran between the 5-acre lots, the houses on them partially hidden by fruit trees and flowering shrubs. The deer must have a field day here in the fall, Lange thought to himself as he walked up on Suleka's Nissan. He moved out into the center of the road, approaching the truck from the passenger side since Too Tall had a reputation for being shy of people he didn't know and Lange didn't want to come up behind him.

"You're done already?" Suleka remarked, having seen Lange approach through her rear view mirror. Too Tall glided away from the Nissan without acknowledging Lange and slowly swayed his way down the road towards the Haddock place.

"For now," Lange replied. He slipped into the seat next to Suleka and pulled the seat belt down over his chest. Suleka watched him, wondering what he was expecting to happen next, which prompted Lange to turn and give her a big, boyish grin. "Can you take me to Marblemount?"

"Why? What's in Marblemount?"

"The Ranger Station. I need to question some of Haddock's co-workers."

"Only if I can come in with you and listen to you question them."

"Will you take notes?"

"No. But I'll pay attention." Now it was Suleka's turn to grin at Lange. "After I've been to the bathroom. That's the real reason I want to go inside." She turned on the engine, pulled forward then backed into the driveway she'd parked alongside.

"I thought you said earlier that you were going home?"

"Mmmm," muttered Suleka. "I changed my mind."

Lange didn't say anything, He'd been left by a spouse too and remembered not wanting to go home to the sound of emptiness. He glanced again at the Haddock house as they drove past; the gray paint of the board and batting exterior, the burgundy trim, the dark green, asphalt shingle roof. It all looked so tidy. Too tidy. Maybe the neighbor had wanted to tarnish that tidiness once and for all. Lange glanced back in an attempt to check the mutual property line for evidence of the disagreement – a dead car, a burn barrel, rusted barbed wire - but it was too late. Suleka had already driven them around two curves in the road and was pointing them towards Sauk Mountain once more.

*****

Suleka turned right at the store in Rockport and put her foot down on the accelerator to gain speed on the highway. Lange took his eyes off the road and let them skim the surface of the Skagit, its glacial waters an inviting ice green in the heat of the afternoon sunshine. It looked so calm but Lange knew it was moving with a force not to be challenged.

"Too Tall told me that one of the neighbor's saw a man going into Haddock's house late last night," Suleka said, interrupting his thoughts.

Lange kept his eyes on the river. "Which neighbor? Because if it was the neighbor that Frankie Deller is questioning right now…."

"No it was the neighbor on the other side of Haddock. Too Tall had just come from his place, which is how come I caught him at the end of that driveway."

"How late last night?"

"'Bout ten-thirty."

"And this neighbor just happened to be looking out at that time?" Lange wasn't really interested. He was remembering the time he saw a group of elk bathing in the Skagit River and wondering how he'd go about calculating the muscle mass required to stand against such a current.

"It was July 4th!" remonstrated Suleka. "The neighbor was setting off fireworks for his kids when this guy pulled in next door and walked up to the front porch."

"So maybe Dinah Haddock had July 4th firework plans too."

"With the boss she's suing for sexual harassment?"

Now she had his interest. Lange turned to look at Suleka. "That's who was there?"

"That's what the neighbor thought. He could see his Ranger uniform in the porch light."

Lange chewed on this for a moment.

The noise of the dog barking became more intrusive as they traveled upriver and Suleka rolled up her window against it. "It's a wonder that mutt's got any yap left," she griped.

"I suppose it could be a different dog."

"That's the same bark we heard back at the store," Suleka stressed, "and the same bark I heard for half the night last night!"

Suleka lived on the other side of the river, almost directly across from where they were now. Lange could imagine the dog's bark echoing unremittingly across the water. No wonder she didn't want to go home.

He blinked his eyes away from the river, swung around, leaned forward and squinted across Suleka to look out her side of the front window. "Osbensky told me that there's an old mule trail up Sauk Mountain that comes out somewhere along the road this way."

"Not along the highway it doesn't."

"No?"

"No. It comes out on the Mayer Road."

"He said you'd know it," Lange informed her.

"Well I know *of* it. I mean I've heard about it. But no one ever uses it anymore. In fact, I'm not sure it even exists anymore. I just know the people that own the land at the end of it because they're family."

Lange looked at her, surprised. "Osbensky said they were Skagit Indians."

"They are."

"I thought you were from Canada."

"I am. But I'm also part Indian."

"Not Skagit Indian."

"No," she agreed, tossing her long braid over her shoulder. "But

I've sat with them at their pow-wows and that makes me family."

Lange dismissed this claim with a surreptitious roll of his eyes as he looked out the passenger window beside him once more.

"Don't mock," warned Suleka.

"How was I mocking?!" He sounded suitably wounded.

"You were rolling your eyes."

Lange pouted. "You don't know that."

"Sure I do,"

"How?"

Suleka gave him a self-satisfied smile. "It's the part of me that's Indian."

Lange wrinkled out a smile; she'd trumped him there. He came back to the subject at hand. "You're sure nobody uses that trail anymore?"

"Why would they? The other trail is much easier. And quicker." Suleka flexed her brows towards him, remembering something. "But I do know that Skagit Land Trust recently bought the area where the trail comes out." She frowned. "Or maybe they bought the land the trail is on. Or part of it." She shook her head. "I'm not sure. I just know the Land Trust raised the money to buy some chunk of real estate in the vicinity of the old trail to protect it and maybe open it up again for use."

Lange chewed on this information as they drove past the farm stand, its parking lot crammed with vehicles belonging to tourists eager for some fresh-made, berry ice cream on this sweltering summer day. Here the river was close enough that Lange could see the rocks and pebbles in its bed and he wished he were standing in it, like the elk, instead of heading up to Marblemount to interrogate suspects in a murder investigation. "Can you take me to where that old trail comes out?" he asked with a gentleness outside his usual tone. He was concerned that he may have offended Suleka with his eye rolling, and the last thing he wanted to do was offend Suleka.

"Maybe on the way back," she agreed.

They rode the rest of the way in silence, past the resort and the winery, the fields and the ranches, on up to a place where dwellings began to get closer together on both sides of them and the speed limit dropped to one synonymous with other small towns spanning the highway. Suleka slowed the Nissan and turned left onto Ranger Station Road. "Are you ready for this?" she asked.

"For what?"

"To come out of retirement and start questioning people again."

Lange bit his lips together. That question didn't interest him.

"What are you going to ask?"

"You'll find out."

"Did you bring a notebook?"

"Didn't need to. You said you'd remember."

"Can I ask a question or two?"

"Nope."

Suleka frowned. She'd ask questions all right. Just not in front of Lange. She bounced the Nissan down the road, wound it around a tear drop shaped, masonry island holding the sign announcing Marblemount Ranger Station and pulled into a parking spot outside the wilderness information center. Lange looked at the single-story building, with its brown metal roof and dark brown wood exterior. To the right of the door was a rust-colored metal sculpture of a tree. A Douglas fir tree, Lange thought to himself.

As he stared at the sculpture, he noticed someone pushing down a slat in the blind at the window next to it. Maybe one of the rangers was waiting for his arrival. Or waiting for an interrogation. "Do you know what Martin French looks like?" he asked Suleka, without taking his eyes off the sculpture.

She thought for a moment. She was pretty sure she did but she was tired. It was warm in the Nissan and her sleepless night had finally permeated her bloodstream and reached her brain. Her eyes glazed over as they stared at the yellow flowers on one of the Oregon grape bushes growing in front of the building. Even though there were vehicles parked all around the compound, it was quiet. Suleka wanted to yield to her fatigue but she knew if she did, she wouldn't sleep tonight either. "Yes," she said, a little louder than necessary.

"Okay so if he's inside, watch him when I say who I am and why I'm there."

She nodded and they opened their doors in unison. Lange was
five long strides to the front door while Suleka stretched her body to
a stand, her spine popping as she eased the creases out of it, letting
the sun wash warm into her aging bones. She didn't care how
quickly Lange wanted to get inside the Ranger Station, he could
wait.

And he did. He sucked on the bridge in his mouth, waiting
patiently by the main door until she found her pep and moved
towards it. Then he took a hold of the climbing axe door handle,
pulled on it and let Suleka pass in front of him to go inside the
building.

They stepped into a large room that had, as its focal point, a
horizontal, 3D topographical map of the North Cascades for people
to walk around and get an aerial view of the mountains and trails.
To the right of that was a couch and a passport stamping station,
where a female ranger was entering the logo of the North Cascades
for a couple of visitors in their National Parks passports. A second
female ranger was stocking brochure holders in a partition wall
between the passport station and a bear display on the opposite side
of the topographical map. Lange made a beeline towards her. As he
did so, Suleka noticed a movement to her left. She turned and saw a
slight, bald headed man in a forest green ranger uniform rise up from
behind a counter. He was about her age with tired eyes and a gentle
countenance. He smiled softly in her direction.

"My name's Callum Lange," she heard Lange say to the young
ranger. "And I'm investigating the murder of Dinah Haddock."

Suleka watched Martin French slip out a door at the far end of
the counter.

* * * * *

"Callum!" Suleka hissed. Lange crossed the room in three steps.
She tipped her head forward, pointed her index finger across her left
breast and muttered through the side of her mouth, "Martin French
just skipped out that way."

Lange looked down the counter towards the door. He didn't

want to leave the young rangers to confer now that they knew his mission but experience told him it was better to go after the one on the run. "Okay, find out how they felt about Haddock," he told Suleka, nodding towards the young women by the passport stamping station, "and ask where they were last night."

"Can do," she muttered, then straightened up a little further, strutting the importance of her task.

Lange didn't notice. He punched open the door that French had used for his exit and stormed through it. He never wondered how he was going to give chase to someone he didn't know by sight; he just had to look for the one running.

But apparently this time he was wrong. For almost as soon as Lange got to the open conference area on the other side of the door, he heard a calm voice ask, "Are you looking for me?"

Lange's head spun first to the workstations on his left then into an office on his right. When he didn't see anybody, he hustled around the conference table and looked into an office on the opposite wall. There he found a man, standing with his back to the door. A man who appeared to be staring out a window at the mountains in the distance, one hand in his pants pocket, the other wrapped around a small, paper cup.

"Are you Martin French?"

"I am."

He turned around and Lange saw a man who looked a little like a Bassett hound with his wrinkled skin and soulful brown eyes, yet French met the ex-detective's gaze without shame.

"I thought you skipped out on us."

French chuckled. "I wouldn't have stood a chance. Your legs are way longer than mine. Plus I've really no need to run. You want some water?"

"Is that what you're drinking?"

French nodded. "Don't want to dry up when you questioned me."

Lange observed the little man some more; was he telling him something about his anxiety level with that remark? Maybe not because there seemed to be a complete peace about him, suggesting he was either very cool under pressure or he really had nothing to hide. "Sure, I'd take some."

The ranger walked past Lange back out into the conference area, pulled another Dixie cup out of a dispenser and filled it from the water cooler. Lange surreptitiously examined the back of French's pants, from the knees down, then glanced around the walls of the office. There was nothing personal on them making him wonder who worked in here as he listened to the water glug glug the vacuum out of its mass. French came back into the office and handed the water to Lange.

"Thank you." Lange looked down at the clear, cold liquid and decided not to beat around the bush. "Why don't you tell me about your relationship with Dinah Haddock," he said.

"I was her boss."

"That's all?"

"Uh huh."

Callum Lange pushed his thick, white hair off his forehead and turned his blue eyes, like interrogation lights, full on Martin French. "Yet you went to see her at her house late last night."

French held his breath for just a second, enough that Lange noticed, but he never broke eye contact with the detective. "I did. Yes."

"Because you had a work related matter to discuss with her?"

"Because I wanted to try and talk to her about this silly sexual harassment thing."

"Silly?"

"I said she looked cute in her uniform one day. For that she was going to file a complaint against me?!"

Lange nodded, as if in agreement. "And last night you two talked about it?"

"No. Last night she left me begging on the front porch while she stood, where I could see her through the window, talking on the telephone in a way that implied she was calling the police," blurted French. Then his whole upper body made a definite move down, as if he'd been holding his breath up tight to his throat while he said what he said and now he could release it. His voice became soft again. "It was probably just as well the door was between us because I felt like doing something I'd regret."

"And did you?"

"Did I what?"

"Do something you regret?'

"Oh. You mean did I kill her?" Lange didn't answer; he watched the ranger's physique remain completely at ease, as if unbothered by the question. "I'm a Buddhist, Mr. Lange," he said, then offered a self-deprecating smile. "Or maybe I should say I'm an aspiring Buddhist, because I don't actually think I'm good enough to call myself a Buddhist. But I do try to live by the philosophy of 'do no harm.' And through my meditation practice I've learned to let the negative wash past me so I won't get sucked in." He looked away, reflecting as he sipped some water, then turned his soulful brown eyes back on Lange. "I will admit that Ms. Haddock could undermine that ability in me but no, I didn't kill her."

"Did she end up letting you in?"

"Uh uh. No. I could see by the way she was watching me out of the side of her eyes that she was just daring me to make a mistake so I walked away." He threw back the last of his water, crumpled the paper cup and moved around Lange to throw it in a bin next to the desk in the office. "Dinah was like a spider, weaving elaborate webs for her various prey but strangely enough I didn't get the impression she was actually planning to trap anyone in those webs. It was more like she was goading us to throttle her with them." He swung around to face Lange again. "That's probably a poor choice of words, isn't it?"

"Throttle?" Lange gave a shrug of his shoulders, not wanting to reveal information about the murder.

French grimaced. "See, and that in itself galls me. That she could make me think like that." He propped his buttocks on the edge of the desk and crossed his legs at the ankles. Lange looked down at his pants once more. Now he could see the mark. When he looked up, French was staring at him. "But that doesn't mean I would ever have acted on those thoughts and tried to hurt her. And it certainly doesn't mean I wanted her dead. Whoever did this is missing the point."

"Which is?"

"That Dinah Haddock was in more pain alive than she is dead. But the pain for the murderer has only just begun."

Lange had seen too many cold-eyed murderers to agree with French's statement but he did know what he meant. And with a victim like Haddock, who could twist the knife so mercilessly in others, Lange could imagine that someone would lose it with her and then live to regret it. But Haddock's murder had every sign of having been planned, which would suggest a killer cool enough not to be plagued with remorse. He tossed back his water and threw the paper cup in the bin. "Do you have another uniform here at the compound?" he asked French.

The ranger walked around the desk. "I think I might have one, yes." He pulled open a drawer and held up a neatly folded uniform. "Here," he announced, then dropped the uniform on the desk in front of Lange. "You can borrow it if you like but I'm pretty sure my pants won't be long enough for you."

"No, no." Lange shook his head. "I don't want that uniform. I want the pants you're wearing."

French tugged at the loose, cotton fabric on one of the legs. "But these are the same length," he argued,

The room had an unnatural, false air feel to it, despite being up against a rain forest steeped in photosynthesis, and Lange had a sudden urge to bolt.

"We need the pants to help us with our inquiries."

"Really?!" Now French looked down at his regulation pants. "They're not trained to answer questions, you know."

Lange ignored the humor. "They were the ones you were wearing yesterday evening, am I right?"

"Well I was wearing them on my way home from work, yes, because I wore this uniform yesterday, But I wasn't wearing them when I went to Haddock's place, if that's what you're implying."

Now Lange looked at French with renewed interest; if he could lie so unflinchingly maybe the rest of his calm demeanor was just an act. "You were seen, Mr. French."

"I might have been seen but I wasn't seen in my uniform," insisted French.

"The neighbor who was setting off fireworks at 10:30 looked across and saw the dark green pants and shirt under the porch light."

"Ah." French gave a self-satisfied smile. "Maybe we should have started with what time was I at Haddock's house? I wasn't there at 10:30. I was there at 8:00."

Lange paused. "Can you prove that?"

French thought for a moment. "When I got to the end of her driveway to leave, at exactly 8:06 – I know because I looked at the clock on my dash, wondering how long it had taken for Dinah's little act to humiliate me into leaving - I had to wait for Katie Schmitt to cross in front of me before I could pull out. She lives on the Harmony Ranch Road and was out for a walk with her dog. She looked me right in the eye and waved."

Damn, thought Lange.

"Do you still need my pants?" asked French. His calm now had a breezy edge to it.

"Where were you at 10:30?"

"Watching the fireworks display at the high school in Concrete. I can give you the names of the people I stood next to. Even spoke to." More like a cocky edge.

"Then who was in a ranger uniform at Haddock's place at 10:30?"

Martin French placed his fingertips on top of the desk in front of him and leaned forward. "Who indeed?" he said.

*****

Callum Lange pushed open the back door of the wilderness information center and sucked in a generous gulp of air like a fish surfacing from water. Had he lost his touch here or what? How come he hadn't started by asking Martin French what time he went over to Haddock's house? Come to that, why hadn't he asked French where he was between midnight and 2 a.m., when the murder had taken place. In fact, why was it that he *still* hadn't asked French that question? After all, it didn't really matter what French was doing at 10:30 last night; it mattered what he was doing between midnight and 2:00 a.m.. He could have visited Haddock at 8:00 p.m., let her push his buttons as he admitted she had, then gone home and planned her murder.

Lange stepped forward, letting the door to the center close behind him. He walked towards a group of stout, big leaf maple trees. He could feel the heat of the day beating down on him but at least out here he could breathe. If there was one thing he didn't do well anymore, it was small, enclosed spaces. That was one of the reasons he'd settled on a thirty-foot diameter yurt pending his log home; a trailer would have felt oppressive.

He stopped before he reached the trees, tipped his face up to the sun and took three long, slow breaths, expanding his chest to full capacity with each one. Now that he thought about it he should have taken that little tidbit of information Suleka dropped on him right back to the neighbor who was the source and asked him exactly what he saw last night at the Haddock house. If he saw somebody in a Park Service uniform standing on the porch at 10:30 pm then maybe he saw – or heard – a car pulling in between midnight and 2:00. Nighttime was usually very quiet in the Upper Skagit and the unexpected sound of a car door closing could set off dogs. Or maybe the neighbor happened to be up in the wee hours and, through a chance glance out his upstairs window, saw a figure moving across the pasture behind Haddock's house. Lange sucked softly on the plastic bridge in his mouth, liberating a tiny section of wild dewberry from his morning snack. His taste buds tingled at the fruity sharpness and his stomach ached with the realization that the only things he'd eaten today were the tiny berries and a banana.

Repressing his sudden hunger he wracked his brain to remember the word French had used. Galled, that was it. It galled Lange that he hadn't thought of these questions sooner. But then he had presumed that Detective Deller's underlings had canvassed the neighborhood. How come she didn't mention what the neighbor saw? Lange shook his head from side to side; he could blame his shortcomings every which way but the truth was he'd fallen prey to local gossip. And he should have remembered just how much the flavor of that gossip changed when it passed from mouth to mouth.

Revitalized, Lange strode back towards the wilderness information center and tugged on the back door. It didn't open. It must have locked automatically when he let it close behind him.

He followed the building around to the front and pulled open the main entry door. Suleka was still in the visitor area, chatting amicably with the two young rangers, and now there were four hikers leaning over the 3D map of the North Cascades. Lange strode the length of the counter to the left, hoping to slip out the door at the end of it before Suleka spotted him. He was eager to hear what she'd learned from Haddock's co-workers but he was also anxious to get back to the crime scene and find out what exactly people had seen and when. And he couldn't do that until he had Martin French's pants.

Two paces from the door, he leaned forward to open it and was startled when it swung towards him, nearly knocking him in the face. Martin French stepped into the room. "Here you go," the ranger said, holding out the pants he'd been wearing.

Lange took them even though he was pretty sure testing them was moot at this point. "Did you happen to go fishing yesterday?" he asked the ranger.

"I dipped my pole in Jackman Creek on the way home from work last night, yes."

Lange nodded. That would explain it. "Well thanks," he said, tucking the pants under his arm. "I doubt we'll have these long."

French didn't seem concerned. Moving like a man just freed from some time-wasting banality he bounced across the room towards the other rangers, passing Suleka, who was on her way over to Lange.

The ex-detective acknowledged her with a quick flick of his eyebrows but held off conversation by heading out to the Nissan. He was in the passenger seat, buckled up and ready to leave, when Suleka opened her door. She lifted a foot to climb in then put it back down on the ground. "You know what?" she said, almost to herself. "I forgot to go to the bathroom with all that questioning."

Lange fixed on the clock on the dash of the Nissan. It was 1:33 already. "Don't be long," he snipped. "I want to get back and question the neighbor that spoke to Too Tall."

Suleka dropped her head and looked at him over the top of her glasses. "I'll be as long as it takes," she informed him.

Lange watched her walk away then rolled down his window, slipped his tongue under the bridge in his mouth and popped out his false teeth. His mind began to wander. He thought about what French had said, about the killer's pain just beginning. He remembered a sapling Silver fir tree that he'd rescued from an invasive noose of blackberries only to have the tree nearly die on him post-rescue. Maybe French had been right. Haddock had wound herself around somebody out there and now that she was gone, what would happen to that person? Lange hoped they wouldn't have to wait to see who withered in order to find Haddock's murderer.

He thought about the seeds on the side of the couch. How long had they been there? Not more than the night he'd thought at first but now that he had time to go over it, he realized that it depended on the temperature of the room and the position of that arm of the couch relative to the sun. That end of the couch was facing the kitchen so there'd be no question of sun but the room had definitely been warm. Too warm for the seeds to have stayed sticky for more than a few hours? He couldn't be sure. He wondered if Frankie Deller had thought to ask the neighbor she was interrogating whether he'd been some place moist and shady last night. But then why would she? Lange hadn't told her what he suspected because he hadn't been sure, even though he knew it was a heck of a clue if his suspicion was right.

He was startled by the sound of his phone ringing in his shirt pocket. He pulled it out and touched the answer button. "Yes?" he asked cautiously.

"It's Frankie Deller, Lange."

"How'd you get my cell phone number?"

"I called the Ranger Station looking for you and Suleka gave it to me."

"Oh." Such a simple explanation. "Did you find the murder

weapon at the neighbor's house?" he asked before Deller could continue.

"Not hardly!" she scoffed. "I found plenty of knives and the guy told me I could take every one of them if I wanted but he seemed way too gleeful about Haddock's death to make me think he'd done it. Wanted to throw a party. Asked us if we'd like to have a drink, to celebrate. I think the only thing bringing him down was the fact he *hadn't* been the one to do it."

"Well if it's any consolation," said Lange, "I don't think Martin French did it either."

"No?"

"No. He's way too calm to have blood on his hands."

There was silence as they both contemplated where this left them now, then Deller jumped in. "Can you swing by and interview the kids from the fireworks party on the top of Sauk? Seems they became pretty tight lipped at he sight of the uniforms on my deputies."

"But I wanted to…"

"….question the other neighbor. I know. I'm on it."

Lange made a mental note not to tell Suleka everything.

"I'll text you the address where the kids crashed after last night's party. You might have more luck getting information out of them. And it's on your way," Deller added. Then hung up.

The driver's side door opened and Suleka dropped into her seat. She threw her braid over her shoulder, slipped the keys into the ignition and started the Nissan. "Do I have some news for you," she said out of the side of her mouth as she pulled on her seat belt and looked over her shoulder to back up.

"Oh yes?" said Lange. His phone dinged the arrival of a text message and he glanced at the screen absently to see an address on Hwy 20. He felt the Nissan move forward, circling the masonry island at the entrance to the compound. "You remember I want to go by the property where that old mule trail up Sauk comes out?" he muttered without looking up.

"Uh huh," Suleka agreed.

There was something about her composure that made Lange sit up and pay attention. "What?" he encouraged.

She cut her eyes towards him, looking smug. She paused as the Nissan bumped onto Ranger Station Road and the glare of the afternoon sunshine spilled through the windshield, momentarily blinding them, then announced, "Seems our murder victim, Ms. "I'm-so-perfect" Dinah, had a lover."

*****

Suleka turned right off Hwy 20 at the east end of Mayer Road, where a pretty, little white church sat with a view through tall, arched windows up the valley towards Boston Basin and Cascade Pass. "Is the trailhead at this end of the road?" Lange asked, as they passed through the shade created by towering fir trees on either side of the road.

"No, it's closer to the other end. Why?"

"I thought this road didn't go all the way through anymore."

"Because the bridge over the creek blew out during the floods a couple of winters ago?" Suleka shook her head no. "They fixed it."

Lange made a face like this was news to him, then grimaced. "I must not get out enough," he said.

Suleka threw him a withering expression.

"I get out!" he amended for her benefit. "I just don't go places where people go."

"Oh please! We're back to you as Roosevelt, the big game hunter?"

Lange looked suitably disgruntled. "I've never claimed I was a big game hunter like Roosevelt but I do go out looking for deer and other wildlife. And the road access to the critters isn't usually the same as the road access to people. Fortunately."

Suleka let it drop.

"Are you okay?" Lange asked as the Nissan rose and fell over the curvature to the new bridge. She turned and looked at him, curious. "I thought maybe you were upset over something."

"You mean other than the fact that my husband walked out on

me last night, I haven't slept in I don't know how many hours, I'm hungry and the sound of that yapping dog seems to be getting louder?"

She was right; the barking was getting louder. "Okay if that's all it is then we're fine. I thought you were miffed at me for some reason." He turned away and scoured the landscape in behind the trees for signs of the dog.

"I am miffed at you," Suleka admitted.

"For what?!" He spun towards her and stared as she pulled the Nissan over to the right and parked it on the brushy verge under the trees at the side of the road. When she switched off the engine, the barking pulsed into the vehicle and they both rolled up their windows against the noise.

"You didn't seem interested in the least that I found out Dinah had a lover."

"*May* have had a lover!" corrected Lange. "I've already been stung once by uncorroborated gossip. I'm not going down that path again without proof." He pushed the passenger side door into a thicket of salmonberries and snaked his way out of the vehicle.

"Okay," said Suleka, who slipped easily out onto the road on her side and raised her voice to talk to him over the top of the truck. "So you want to verify the information. I get that. But I thought I did a good job questioning them."

"I agree."

"Then why didn't you *say* that?"

"I just did!"

Suleka opened her mouth then closed it. This was pointless. Plus she didn't like having to yell over the dog. She flipped her head to the right just as Lange said. "Where d'you suppose that's coming from?"

"Maybe it's Velma's dog. Velma Noise. She owns the land back in there by the bridge that we crossed. And she's got a chunky, older, Australian shepherd kind of dog that's almost deaf, I guess."

"Why would that make it bark nonstop?"

"I have no idea," she said with a shrug. "I don't know much about dogs. Except that I don't care for them."

Lange flipped his eyebrows up into his forehead and counted to three. "Where's the trailhead?" he asked.

"Oh." Suleka crossed to the left of him and led the way around an arching shrub that was heavy with lilac blossoms into what looked like an overgrown driveway. The land sloped up away from them and a grouping of big boulders, with pale green moss furring their tops, seemed the most logical access into the climb. Suleka swatted a couple of big horse flies away from her face and pointed through the trees. "If you go up through here you come to Barr Creek and you follow along beside that until you reach a waterfall."

"And that's where you access the old mule trail, at the waterfall?"

"No, I don't think so. I think you have to go beyond that before you get to the bottom of the old trail. But you'd have to ask Velma. Her family owns this stretch of land." She hesitated. "I think. I'm pretty sure this is what Skagit Land Trust was negotiating to buy. But they could have bought it already." She shook her head no. "I don't remember. But there's an article about it in the last newsletter I got from them."

Lange stopped bobbing from side to side, trying to see further into the woods, and turned his penetrating blue eyes on Suleka. "You get their newsletters?"

"Uh huh."

His mind raced. "Do they list subscribers in their newsletters?"

"Yep."

"Can I see one?"

"I'd have to go home and get it…"

"Maybe after you drop me back at the crime scene?"

Suleka dropped her chin and gave Lange her best schoolmarm look over the top of her glasses. "I'm guessing there's a reason you want this?" He nodded. "And I'm guessing you're not going to tell me what that reason is?"

Lange sucked in a short, noisy breath. "I'd rather not."

Suleka nodded. "I'm also guessing we're not here just because you're curious."

He threw both hands out at his sides as if this should be obvious.

"Do you hear that dog?"

"Er......YES! And it's not doing my state of mind any good!" She smacked her left forearm then flicked a dead mosquito off it. "How much longer?" she asked.

Lange held up one finger. "Just one more minute," he reassured her. Then he climbed up on one of the boulders and peered in through the trees. "I don't s'pose you have a pair of binoculars in your truck?"

"I do. Yes." He turned and looked at her, surprised. "What? I like to bird watch."

While she walked back to the Nissan, Lange climbed down from the boulder and examined the area they'd been standing in. He ran his eyes over the trees and shrubs that led into this opening then he crouched down and scoured the ground. The small dimension hard rock that had presumably been the edge of the road when it first went in had quack grass growing through it almost everywhere and Lange hoped for a stray footprint or tire track. But nothing revealed itself to him. The ground was just too dry and dusty.

"Here you go," said Suleka, coming up behind him and holding out a pair of binoculars.

"Thanks," replied Lange. He looked up at her from his crouch down by the ground. "Can you call your friend, Velma? Ask if we can go in through this property?"

"I can. Sure."

He stood up and took the binoculars out of her hand. Then waited.

"Well I can't do it now. Her number's on my sheet at home."

Lange's mouth dropped open in a silent oh of acknowledgement. Then with one swift move, he climbed back onto the boulder, adjusted the binoculars to his eyes and moved them over every inch of visible ground through the trees. His head rotated slowly, steadily - and then stopped. Was that something glinting in the sunlight? He moved the binoculars back a few centimeters but nothing revealed itself to him. He climbed up onto the next boulder and craned himself forward, keeping the field glasses steady in the area where he'd seen the sudden twinkle. He waited patiently. A small breeze blew, shifting the branches of the trees just enough that the sunlight streamed through and hit whatever was on the ground, making it glint again. Lange exhaled and lowered the field glasses. He sucked reflectively on the bridge in his mouth as the sound of the barking dog sank deeper and deeper into his consciousness. And then he heard the victim, gasping and struggling every time the knife beat down into her body. Not long now, he promised her in his mind.

"Are you okay?"

Suleka's question clanged into his consciousness. "What? I'm fine."

"Well your cell phone's ringing."

Lange looked down at his shirt pocket and was a little shocked to realize that she was right. He pulled out his phone and answered the call. It was Deller.

"Did you go by and talk to the kids that partied at the top of Sauk last night?"

"I did but they didn't tell me much." He turned to climb down off the boulder and noticed that Suleka was preparing herself to step forward and catch him should be stumble even though she was his senior by a few years. He thought about the expression on her face when she'd been looking for a compliment about her interrogation skills and he added, into the phone, "They opened up more for Suleka. She has an ease with these local people that I don't."

Suleka lifted her chin slightly, like a cat that's laid a mouse at its master's feet, and Lange knew he'd just made points with her.

"They told her that they saw the husband's car at the trailhead. And it was still there when they started their descent around 1:30 a.m.."

"Okay," sighed Deller. "And you're where now?"

"Heading back to the crime scene," replied Lange as he walked around the lilac bush to get back in the Nissan. "Did you identify those seeds yet?"

"Just got the call from the WSU Horticultural Lab. in West Mount Vernon. They are….." She paused, as if making sure she had the pronunciation right. "….Adenocaulon bicolor. Does that mean anything to you?"

"It does," declared Lange, an edge of excitement in his voice. "It means that we now have something that you can use to get us a search warrant."

*****

They rode in silence back down the highway towards Rockport, Lange going over every detail of his conversation with Detective Deller in his mind while Suleka fought to stay awake at the wheel. "Do we have time for me to pull into the store and get some coffee?" she asked as they neared the turn off for Hwy 530.

"Go ahead," said Lange. It really didn't matter what time they got back to the crime scene now; Deller had already questioned the one neighbor about the mysterious, 10:30 p.m. visitor and the search warrant would be a wait. All that was left to do was for Lange to figure out exactly how the murderer had arrived at Haddock's house.

Suleka slowed the Nissan and turned into the paved area in front of the small, country store with its two gas pumps and a 'self-kicking' kiosk, where four boots on criss-cross lengths of pipe could be turned by unsuspecting tourists and kick them in the butt. "I'll be right back," she told Lange as she stepped out of the truck.

He watched her walk towards the wide, grey doors at the front of the building but decided it was too hot to sit in the Nissan and wait. He climbed out, tipped his face up to the sun and let his mind drift away from the buzzing of the highway to his left and towards the wild and scenic river on his right. He began walking, down around the bend in the road, past a tiny, A-frame, silver shingled house, past the entrance to the State Park and along to the river. He stepped around some guardrail and continued forward onto the bridge, walking between two metal railings protecting a narrow strip of sidewalk safe for pedestrians. He stopped and looked down at the teal green water. A couple in a canoe floated downstream underneath him, barely touching their oars to the current. Already Lange felt cooler, as the breeze traveling with that current slipped under his short sleeves and billowed his shirt out, away from his slim torso, He heard a whirring as three bicyclists speed across the bridge behind him. He felt the hair on the nape of his neck stand up. Of course! *That* was how the murderer had traveled to Haddock's house.

He turned and walked the rest of the sidewalk, unconsciously following the cyclists towards Hwy 530. Once clear of the bridge, his stride lengthened and his certainty grew. He glanced left to cross to the other side of the highway, but stopped when he and saw Suleka crawling towards him in the Nissan. "You couldn't have waited the few minutes it took me to get my coffee?" she snipped through the open passenger window as she pulled up alongside him.

"I wasn't thinking," confessed Lange.

Suleka puckered her lips. Of course he wasn't thinking! "Well do you want me to drive you over to Haddock's place or not?" she asked.

"No, you head on home. I need to follow the route."

Suleka opened her mouth to ask, "Which route?" then changed her mind. "Okay," she said and headed off down Hwy 530.

Lange marched to the other side of the road. He looked across a wide, marshy field and spotted a gate leading into it at the end of another section of guardrail. He wondered if this was where the bicyclist had gone off the road, to hide from any middle-of-the night traffic. But the grass in the field was waist high, which would have made crossing it on a bicycle difficult. Too difficult for someone up against a time constraint.

Lange rounded the corner onto the Harmony Ranch Road and lengthened his stride. He tried to focus on the idea of a cyclist pedaling by the light of the moon but became distracted by a small pile of bear scat in the middle of the road. Must not have been a very big bear, Lange thought to himself as he bent over the scat. He examined the undigested pits in the scat; cherries, that's what they looked like. He glanced left then right and saw two cherry trees in a neighboring front yard. That must have been the site of the feast.

He straightened up and continued down the road. Last summer, shortly after he'd first moved out to the Skagit, Lange came around a corner on Sauk Mountain and startled a black bear eating wild blueberries on the hillside. The bear skittered down into the road and faced Lange. Lange took one step back; the bear took one step forward. Lange swallowed hard. That obviously hadn't worked. He thought for a second, wondering how to deal with this situation given that he was unarmed, and then he did the only other thing he could think to do; he stepped forward, towards the bear. The animal tipped his nose up into the air, caught a whiff of human, turned tail and ran.

Lange smiled at the memory as he noticed a narrow, dirt path heading away from the road. On a hunch, he followed it. It went straight for about 200 yards, curled around behind a large house and barn, then ended in a field of straggly, dried out grasses and weeds. Lange knew that he must be on private property but decided against turning back. He pushed on through the browned grass, looking for that one thin trail that would suggest a bicycle had come through, but he didn't find it.

He stopped, sure that he hadn't looked hard enough – or in the right place – and doubled back. He found the end of the footpath again and this time continued straight, moving further away from the houses before looping to the right, in the direction of the Haddock place. The sun was beating down on the field and the only sound Lange could hear was the sound of his pants scuffing against the tall grasses as he lifted one foot after another over the rugged terrain. Tiny trickles of sweat ran down his back on the inside of his shirt but Lange paid them no heed. He was too focused on finding something, anything that would lend credence to what he was sure of in his gut.

It wasn't until he got to the pasture behind Haddock's house that he found what he'd been looking for; a single, skinny, bicycle tire track. He even found a patch of flattened grasses, indicative of the bike being tossed to one side while the murderer went into the house and did the deed. But he couldn't for the life of him find where the bike had come into the pasture.

Lange doubled back again and again, turning circles in the sticky, oppressive, afternoon heat to no avail. He went back to Haddock's pasture and bent over the trail for the umpteenth time. Sure enough it came and went through the dusty, dried out grass but where did it start? He heard a vehicle crunch onto gravel, then a door open and slam closed but he didn't look up. He inched along in a crouch, determined not to let the trail elude him this time, but he got to same place he'd got to a multitude of times this afternoon and it disappeared. Lange pushed his fingers through his thick, white hair, mystified.

"D'you find something?" he heard from behind him.

Lange swung around and nearly bumped into Detective Deller. "No!" he said, as he rose to stand next to her. "Well, yes," he amended. "I found a bicycle track, which is how I think the killer came to the house. But I can't figure out how it came into the pasture."

"Maybe our perp just cycled up the driveway."

Lange's eyes bugged open. He looked over Deller's shoulder at the wide expanse of graveled driveway. Of course! The killer didn't need to be fancy about approaching the house; just surreptitious about not setting off the motion sensor light on the front porch by coming in through the front door. So pedaling up the driveway and into the pasture, to dump the bike where it wouldn't be seen, made total sense. Why hadn't he thought of that? "Any word on the search warrant?" was all he said to Deller.

She handed him the piece of paper she'd been holding behind her back and grinned.

"Already?!"

"I called on Judge Wisman," Deller explained. "He was very sympathetic."

Lange was impressed. He wished he'd had such judges in New York. He opened the paper and read it quickly. It included all personal effects, which is what he'd wanted. "Good," he said, handing the warrant back to Deller. "Any word on when the husband might get down here from Sauk Mountain?"

Deller nodded. "Deputy Collins called me about 15 minutes ago and said they were just leaving the parking lot."

Lange turned and looked at the broad, thickly forested ridge that formed the backbone of Sauk Mountain. "What time is it now?" he asked.

"Almost 4:20."

Lange chuckled. "I spent almost 2 hours searching the land behind the adjacent properties for signs of a bike and all the time the killer came up the driveway."

"That's retirement for you," said Deller. "You're not thinking like a criminal anymore."

Lange nodded. She was right. He'd been thinking like a black bear when he'd followed the road less traveled. Criminals were lazy.

They heard Suleka's Nissan chugging down the road towards them and watched as she pulled into the driveway and parked. She climbed out of the truck, flapping a document of some kind in the air as she walked towards them. "I've got the newsletter," she announced with a trill, "and Velma said she'd leave the gate open for us so we could access her property." She came up alongside Lange and handed him the newsletter. Then looked at him over the top of her glasses. "She was kind of curious why you wanted to go in there though."

Lange didn't say anything. He opened the Skagit Land Trust newsletter and stared at a page.

Suleka looked over his shoulder. "Did you find what you were looking for?"

"I did," he replied and folded up the newsletter.

"I hope you're right about this, Callum," said Frankie Deller. "Because we're wasting valuable time if you're not."

"I'm right," said Lange looking up at Sauk one more time. "And pretty soon we'll have the proof that I'm right."

*****

It was exactly 5:02 p.m. when the grey, Ford Explorer with the gold Sheriff insignia pulled into the driveway. Lange watched through the front window as Haddock's husband climbed out of the passenger side. He was 33, 34 maybe, with impeccably groomed dark hair and just a dusting of overnight shadow on his well-sculpted jaw line. His legs, what could be seen of them below his light gray shorts, were muscular, suggesting he hiked a lot, although his top-of-the-line hiking boots looked barely worn. He hoisted a heavy backpack onto his right shoulder without losing an ounce of his composure. Only his eyes looked troubled.

Deputy Collins came around from the driver's side and in contrast to the husband looked ruddy faced and sweaty. He put a friendly hand on the husband's free arm and led him up to the porch.

Lange turned slightly, Detective Deller to his right, Suleka somewhere in the background, and watched as the handle on the front door rotated. "Mr. Haddock," he greeted the young man.

The husband looked at him, perplexed. He let his pack slide down off his shoulder and thud to the floor just inside the front door. "I'm Brian Bowlds," he explained. "It's my wife that's called Haddock." He paused and Lange could tell that he was thinking about what he'd just said. "Was called Haddock," he corrected quietly. He turned away and his eyes immediately fell to the bloodstains on the floor. Pain flashed across his face as he took an involuntary step forward. "Is that where she.....?"

Deller blocked his path. "Mr. Bowlds, we're very sorry for your loss..."

Bowlds looked at her like he didn't understand. The color slowly drained out of his cheeks and Detective Deller stretched out her right arm as if to catch him. "Would you like to sit down, Brian?" she asked.

He swallowed hard and shook his head no. "I just want you to tell me what happened to my wife," he whispered.

"We will," Deller assured him. "But first we'd like to ask you a few questions."

Lange jumped in. "Can you tell us what time exactly you hiked up Sauk Mountain yesterday?"

Again Bowlds looked perplexed. "Why?" he questioned.

"We're trying to establish who saw Dinah last," explained Deller.

"The murderer. Obviously."

"No, we mean who saw her before she was murdered."

"Well it wasn't me. I worked until 3:00 in the afternoon, came home, grabbed my pack and headed up Sauk. Dinah was out."

"What time did you get down to the lake?" pressed Lange.

"I don't know. Sometime early in the evening."

"Did you pass anyone on the trail?"

Bowlds threw his arms out and stepped back, nearly elbowing Deputy Collins in the stomach as he did so. "Why?! How is knowing that going to help you catch my wife's murderer?" Neither Lange nor Deller answered, presenting Bowlds with flat, impassive stares. Bowlds sighed dejectedly as he yielded to their question. "Did I pass anyone on the trail?" he repeated. "Yes, there were maybe two groups of hikers coming down the trail but I was alone by the time I got to the top and alone when I hiked down into the lake."

"Until the kids showed up," added Lange. He watched Bowlds very carefully but didn't see any reaction to his assertion.

"The kids?"

"You didn't hear them setting off fireworks from the top of Sauk after dark?"

"I was asleep after dark," he said, with a wry smile. "And I wore ear plugs to avoid being disturbed by the sound of fireworks."

"You'll have those ear plugs in your pack then?" asked Deller and Lange commended her mentally for jumping on the opening.

"Sure. Yes. I guess," stuttered Bowlds, touching the pockets of his shorts as if they might be in there. His brow furrowed. "Why? D'you want to see them?"

"Actually we want to see everything in your pack, Mr Bowlds, and have a search warrant allowing us to do so." Frankie Deller flapped open the search warrant and held it out to Bowlds.

Bowlds nostrils flared, the only sign that he didn't like the turn this conversation had taken. "Really? You're treating me like a suspect when I was up on Sauk Mountain?"

When Deller and Lange didn't reply again, Bowlds snatched the warrant out of Deller's hand and pointed to his pack. "Go for it," he conceded. "But now, if you don't mind, I think I will sit down."

Bowlds stepped forward again, as if to go further into the room, but Deller stood firmly in his way. Lange didn't like the claustrophobic feeling he was getting from them all being huddled by the front door but he knew that Deller's plan in cornering Bowlds was to rattle his calm. And Lange was eager to see what this man looked like when his calm was rattled. "Of course," Deller replied. "Deputy Collins will fetch you a seat."

The rhythmic, heavy breathing that Collins had been adding to the background suddenly stopped, as the Deputy realized he was being called upon to do something. He squeezed out from behind Bowlds and lumbered into the bedroom, re-emerging a few seconds later with a straight-backed chair. He placed it snug up against the wood-shelving unit around the fireplace insert and repositioned himself in the doorway to the bedroom. Bowlds carefully moved the chair away from the shelving unit and ran his fingers over the wood, as if checking for scratches. Then he swung around and sat down. He leaned forward, his knees spread apart, feet together, and rested his forearms on his thighs to read the search warrant, seemingly oblivious to the fact that Lange and Deller had both slipped on plastic gloves and shifted his backpack to a spot on the floor between them.

"You need me to do anything?" Suleka asked over Lange's shoulder.

Lange tugged the black, bolster-like stuff sack out from under the backpack straps and glanced at Deller. She nodded. He handed it off to Suleka. "Yes. Pull the sleeping bag out of this and spread it out."

"Okay," she replied. "What are we looking for?"

Lange glared at her. She popped both eyebrows up in response and tapped the side of her nose. "Got it," she muttered. She took a step back and began liberating the sleeping bag from its tight quarters.

Lange, now down on one knee, snapped open the top of the back and pulled out another stuff sack holding a small set of metal cookware. Lange handed this off to Deller who noticed, as she pulled it apart, how very neat and clean it all looked. "What were you doing. Mr Bowlds, when Deputy Collins arrived at your camp?"

"I was sleeping."

"Is that right. And it was - what? - early afternoon when you got there?" Deller went on, looking directly at Collins.

The deputy had to think about his answer. "Yes," he said finally.

Deller stared pointedly at Bowlds but this time, his look back to her was flat and impassive, as if daring her to question his sleeping habits. She didn't take the bait. She knelt down beside Lange and watched intently as he pulled socks, a fleece jacket, a t-shirt and then some pants out of the pack.

Having found what he was looking for, Lange stood up, and held the pants out in front of him. He slowly turned them around as Deller investigated every inch of them with her eyes. Suleka watched, not really sure what she was supposed to be seeing, but wanting to be part of the process. She glanced at Bowlds, whose eyes remained fixed on the warrant. But when Deller nodded up at Lange, she noticed Bowlds flick his eyes in their direction as if curious about what they were seeing.

"We have our seeds," stated Lange, folding the pants carefully before slipping them into an evidence bag that Deller had handed him.

"Seeds?" queried Bowlds.

"Yes, seeds. The same seeds that we found on the end of the couch where your wife was murdered last night."

Bowlds threw himself back in the chair, his face scrunched up like this didn't make any sense at all. "So? I picked up some seeds when hiking yesterday! Big deal. They're probably everywhere that's brushy around here, which is how come they're in my house and on my pants. That Sauk Mountain Trail is very brushy!"

Lange shook his head no. "These seeds aren't that common. They're found on a plant that needs the damp and that south face of Sauk is very dry."

"Which means what?"

"Which means," declared Lange, "that you hiked down the east face of Sauk Mountain last night and these seeds are the tell-tale evidence that you did so…"

"It also means that you, Brian Bowlds, are under arrest for the murder of your wife," added Detective Deller, pulling a pair of handcuffs out of the back pocket of her black pants as Deputy Collins encouraged Bowlds up out of his seat with a hand under his right armpit.

"You've got to be *kidding* me!" argued Bowlds. "You're using *seeds* as evidence that I murdered my wife?!"

"No, we'll be using the knife you killed her with as evidence that you murdered your wife."

"What knife? I don't see any knife!" Bowlds flinched as Deller cuffed his hands behind his back.

"Not yet you don't," replied Lange. "But I'm pretty sure I know where it is. And when we take you there next, you'll know that I know too."

Bowlds opened his mouth to reply but paused, his demeanor suddenly cagey like he sensed a trap. Detective Deller used his hesitation to read Bowlds his rights, walking him out to put him in the back of her vehicle as she did so. Suleka helped Deputy Collins gather up the contents of the backpack to load into the Ford Explorer. "You riding with me?" she asked Lange before she stepped out the front door.

He nodded. "I'll be just a minute."

Suleka closed the door and Callum Lange swiveled around to listen. He ran his eyes over the couch, the coffee table, the bloodstains on the floor but no sounds of the struggle that ended the victim's life came to him. He nodded, satisfied.

Now all he had to do was quiet a barking dog.

*****

They convoyed from the crime scene to Barr Creek and arrived to find an older lady, with salt and pepper hair and gentle brown eyes, waiting for them at the side of the road.

"Hi, Velma," called Suleka, as she stepped out of the Nissan.

Velma smiled and nodded at her friend, then smiled at Lange.

"I'm Callum Lange," he said, stretching his hand out in her direction.

Velma was holding a tall walking pole, which she switched to her left hand so she could shake. "I know," she said. "Suleka's told me a lot about you. She says I need to tell you some hunting stories."

Lange's interest perked immediately. "You have some?"

"Not me. But my grandsons. Oh boy, they've got some doozies." She laughed and looked past Lange. "Maybe I shouldn't tell you in front of Frankie, though. Might get my boys in trouble."

Lange turned and saw Frankie Deller closing the door to her vehicle and walking towards them. "You know I think your grandsons are great, Velma. How're they doing?"

"Pretty good, thank you. Thanks for asking." She paused and let her eyes wander to Deputy Collins and the man in cuffs he had a hold of by the arm. Lange saw incomprehension flick across her face but not judgment. She probably thought Bowlds looked like a nice young man. She blinked and looked back at Lange. "So you want to go through my property to that old east face trail up Sauk?" she asked.

"If that's okay," he answered.

"Uh huh. It's uphill for about a quarter mile past these rocks," she said, pointing to the flat-topped, moss covered boulders, "before you get to Barr Creek. Then you'll find an old gravel road that my family punched in years ago - it's covered in duff now but you can feel it's hard under the surface – and you take that for another half mile to the Sauk Mountain Trail."

"Do you know whose dog that is?" Lange asked, pointing up the road in the direction of the bark.

"Yeah," Velma admitted. "That's my Moose. I think the fireworks last night really got to him."

"I'm guessing he's on a chain?"

She nodded. "A chain on a run."

"Would you mind letting him off?" asked Lange.

Velma shrugged. "As long as he gets back to me and doesn't go chasing off after some bear."

"We'll get him back to you," promised Lange.

She smiled once more and walked away from them, up the road, limping hard on her right side.

Lange didn't tarry. He bounded across the boulders and started up a narrow trail that went past a hollow filled with ferns, moss and dark green salal leaves, then leveled off alongside an unearthed tree stump that had created the hollow. Here he stopped, crouched down and scoured the land under the trees. The others were making their way up the trail to the rhythm of the dog's constant bark and Lange wished he could find what he was looking for before they reached him. He stood, preparing to step off the trail, and looked down. There it was!

"Did you find it?" asked Detective Deller when she came up behind him. Collins was behind her, walking with Bowlds, and Suleka was in the rear.

Lange pointed down, a few feet from where they were standing. "It's right there. Under those cedar boughs."

Deller turned to Bowlds. "You were so sure we wouldn't catch you, that's all the trouble you took to hide your bike?!"

Bowlds didn't bother to look. "That's not my bike," he said.

And then the dog stopped barking. Everyone looked up, as if expecting it to begin again, but it didn't. Instead there was silence for a few moments, followed by the heavy panting and grunting of a dog charging through the brush. When they finally saw the canine, through the trees, not 100 feet from where they all stood, Lange was surprised. He thought that with a name like Moose he'd see a big dog, like a Mastiff or Rottweiler, but Suleka was right, he was some kind of Australian Shepherd mix. With a big bark.

Lange kept his eyes on the grey and white mutt as he skidded to a halt just shy of the overturned stump and began turning in circles, snuffling frantically at the ground. When he found what he was looking for, he bounded forward, let out a yip of delight and bent to retrieve it.

"No, Moose!" yelled Detective Deller. The dog stopped, lifted his head and cocked it to one side, looking through the trees at Deller with one blue and one brown eye. "Good dog," she cooed. "Sit."

Moose sat.

Deller pulled an evidence bag out of her pants pocket and handed it to Deputy Collins. "Go get what he's found," she said.

Collins opened his mouth as if to argue, then thought better of it. He shuffled past Bowlds and dropped down off the trail, making as wide a circle as he dared around the bicycle given the uneven nature of the terrain. He plowed his way noisily through the undergrowth, reached the dog and stood staring down at the ground as if transfixed.

"What is it?" Deller called out.

"The knife."

"Well pick it up!"

The sound of Collins' adenoidal breathing filled the woods as he pulled the evidence bag over his right hand and leaned forward to pick up the knife. Moose bowed his head over his find and growled. Collins shot back upright. He paused, obviously wondering what to do next, and Moose sat back up, cocking his head inquisitively. Collins reached his right hand forward. When Moose didn't move, Collins bent over quickly. But Moose was quicker. He bowed his head over the knife before Collins could reach it, bared his teeth and growled again.

The sheriff's deputy stood back up and threw Detective Deller a pained look. Frankie rolled her eyes and sighed. She stepped forward, picked up a stick and tossed it into the woods above them. Moose immediately gave chase. Collins grabbed the knife and hightailed it clumsily back through the trees before the dog returned.

"Take that down to the Explorer and call forensics to come and do their thing," Deller told him when he reached the trail. Then she turned to Bowlds. "Now would be a good time to make a statement," she informed him.

"I was camped up at Sauk Lake last night," he said simply.

"Your *tent* was camped up Sauk Lake," corrected Lange. "And I expect you hung out in it until about 8:00 p.m., when you felt sure nobody else would arrive at the lake for the night. Then you made your way to the east face trail, that you'd learned about through your membership in Skagit Land Trust, hiked down to here in about four or five hours, retrieved the bicycle that you'd hidden just like it is now and biked over to your place to murder your wife. Once the deed was done, you cycled back here, hid the bike again, tossed the bloody knife into the woods, which the dog saw, or probably heard and smelled, and started barking to be let off the chain to retrieve it, while you hiked another four or five hours back up into the lake. It was a long, arduous night for you, which is why you were sleeping when Deputy Collins came to fetch you this afternoon."

"I don't even know where the east face trail is," shrugged Bowlds.

"Oh but you do," countered Lange. "And you have the seeds on your pants to prove it." He nodded at Deller, who took Bowlds by the arm and started leading them further up the trail. Moose joined them, trotting alongside Deller with the stick in his mouth.

They came to Barr Creek, which was gushing boisterously over the ledges in her bed, and found the old road Velma had told them about. This they followed through a grouping of skinny, alder trees, evidence of a previous mudslide, to a shady glade where the unmaintained trail up Sauk began.

"Wait!" said Lange and stepped ahead of Deller to observe the green growth that had taken over the old mule trail. He nodded at what he was seeing and then knelt down and slipped his right hand under a low-growing, triangular shaped leaf that was one of many on the trail. "This," he said, "is Adenocaulon bicolor, so named because the top of the leaf is bright green while the underside," he said, flipping the leaf over, "is silvery. Because it's a large leaf on a weak stalk, it turns over easily when somebody walks past it." He paused, letting go of the leaf and standing up. "The common name for this plant is Pathfinder because hikers can find their way back out of the woods if they follow the trail of leaves that they turned over on the way in." Lange pointed at a silvery line running through the green growth on the side of the mountain, an indication of somebody having traveled this route recently. "It also has seeds which are said to "trail" hikers by sticking to the bottom of their pants when they walk through them." He looked at Bowlds with his piercing blue eyes. "I don't think we're going to have any trouble proving you made this trek last night."

His pronouncement must have riled Bowlds because, in a single breath, the young man lost control of his calm and made it seem as if the skin on his face had peeled back to reveal the monster within. "You don't know what it was like," he spat, "living with that woman! That woman that had to have everything the way *she* wanted it! Down to the last, teeny-tiny, excruciating detail." His chest heaved and an angry sob escaped unbidden from between his lips. "And then to discover that she was *cheating* on me….!"

Lange and Deller made eye contact; the 10:30 p.m. visitor. They waited, to see if he would say more, but Bowlds bit back his anger just as quickly as he had vented it, dropped his head and let himself be led away by Deller and Moose.

Lange looked across at Suleka. Her eyes were glazed over as she stared off into nothingness.

"It's cool here," she muttered.

Lange nodded. "It's in the shade."

She blinked across at him. "I think I might stay awhile."

He smiled, trying to draw the sadness out from inside her.

"I guess I just don't want to go home now that my husband's not there to cook for," she admitted.

Lange started down the trail. "Talking of cooking," he said. He stopped and looked back at Suleka. "I was thinking we might barbecue those steaks you got me from the Double O Ranch on the gas grill I set up next to my log pile."

"Do you have barbecue sauce?"

"No, but I have other seasonings." He turned and continued down the trail.

Suleka began to follow. "D'you need me to pick up some wine?"

"I have whiskey."

She smiled and looked up at the sky. "Even better."

From

How to Make a Pot in 14 Easy Lessons
a novel

Nicola Pearson

www.howtomakeapotin14easylessons.com

Lesson 1

Gather the Love

When deciding whether or not you want to make pots, you should first determine if you have the love. Otherwise there's really no point in getting your hands dirty.

Joe felt the sun on his broad shoulders as he leaned forward to assess the wet clay. He could tell by how shiny it was just how much longer it would have to sit before it was dry enough to use but he'd been muddying his hands in wet clay as a potter for 13 years now and he was still drawn to touch it whenever he could. He pushed against the sticky material with his right hand, evening out the thickness at one end of the long drying tray and then decided to do the same for the other end with his left hand.

He didn't have to do this. He had a perfectly adequate dough mixer sitting inside his studio that he used for making clay; but this clay had been trimmings from another potter who didn't make his own clay and, rather than waste it, he had brought it to Joe to throw in his mixer. But when Joe examined the trimmings he found dog hair and gravel and other impurities from the floor of the other guy's studio so he threw the trimmings into a blunger with an excess of water. The blunger, an oversized eggbeater, spun the two materials to a homogenous, creamy consistency, which Joe then poured through a kitchen sieve onto a cloth that he had laid on insulating firebricks in this wooden drying tray. He set the whole works on sawhorses alongside his garden and between the soft, porous firebricks absorbing the moisture and the heat of the sun, the clay was in the ideal place to dry. This was a labor of love.

It was also one of the best ways to make clay in Joe's opinion. Overwetting it and spinning it in a blunger, then leaving it to settle and dry in the sun meant the clay particles were more evenly dispersed than they would be in a clay mixer, creating a finished product with greater plasticity. Just the way he liked it for throwing. He'd make all his clay this way except it rained so darned much in the Upper Skagit he couldn't be sure he'd ever get it dry. So he only did it this way when he was recycling somebody else's clay and then only in the summer months. June was even a little early for this method but the last few days had brought cloudless, sunny skies and so Joe had jumped at the chance to get these trimmings dealt with.

He looked at his hands; they were covered in a thick, grayish coating of clay. He clicked twice in the side of his cheek and Magnolia, who had been rubbing her back in the sweet June grass a few feet away, flipped onto her paws and trotted over to see what was needed. Joe bent down and pressed a hand into each side of the brown dog's belly.

"There's a good girl," he told her and Maggie wagged her tail happily and pushed her nose up into his face. "Don't slime my glasses," he warned her before standing back to admire his handiwork. Satisfied, he looked at his dog and said, "Okay, let's go get our girl some irises."

~

Lucy looked out the window of the plane and let her eyes stare over the expanse of gray tarmac at Kennedy International Airport. The plane had taxied away from the gate towards the runway almost 20 minutes ago and they still hadn't taken off. The pilot came onto the overhead speakers; "Another five minutes, folks, and we'll be on our way." The man sitting next to Lucy tipped his head down towards her and scrunched up his face. "They train them to lie, you know," he told her.

Lucy flashed him an amused look with her green eyes and smiled but then she turned away, not wanting to get drawn into a conversation. She just wanted to sit and think about being with Joe.

She was so excited to see him again after four months of them being apart but she had some other emotion going on at the same time. Fear, maybe? Lucy Carson was twenty-seven and had left her native England for France when she was twenty-two, then left France for New York City when she was twenty-four, in the hopes of doing theatre in as many places around the world as possible so she could go back to England and open her own theatre using the best of what she'd learned elsewhere. But now she was moving to Washington State, a place that had never been on her theatrical itinerary, and she was doing it for a man! She'd never moved anywhere for a man before and some part of her didn't really believe she was doing it now, particularly since she had no intention of settling down and getting married. But Joe had a special quality about him, a warm gravitational pull that made Lucy unable to resist drifting in his direction and she sensed that she might never meet anyone like him again. So despite her promise to herself never to get entangled in love, she found herself putting her theatrical journey on hold for a while and letting her heart take center stage.

As appealing as that prospect seemed every time Lucy pictured herself with Joe, she also knew there was something about this move that was bothering her because she'd been doing a lot of strange things recently. Like sleeping at weird hours, for long stretches of time. Just last week, she'd gone back to the apartment she shared with her roommate, Frank, around 5 p.m., planning to have a bite to eat and then work on her Master's degree thesis but as soon as she got through the door, she laid down for a moment on the couch and woke up 3 hours later when the telephone rang. It was Joe and he was shocked to find her sleeping at 8 o'clock at night. So was Lucy.

She'd also been forgetting things recently, some of them important things. Like the papers she was supposed to get for her professor from the library. Lucy had been this professor's research assistant for a year now and had never forgotten an assignment he'd given her. "I think I may be anxious about this move," she heard herself telling him to explain her omission.

"I've had that impression," the professor agreed, making Lucy aware that even others could tell she wasn't herself.

Lucy's thoughts were interrupted by the pilot again, who now told them that they were being delayed because of a storm passing across Long Island that they could see if they looked out the windows to their right. Her neighbor, Mr. Tall and Lanky, observed dryly that all he could see was blue skies. Lucy just nodded and smiled. She wasn't really paying attention. She was thinking how ready she was to leave New York and spend more than just a passing vacation with Joe. How much more would depend on whether she could overcome her fears when it came to love. And if she couldn't, well, as Joe had told her with his winning charm, at least Washington State was closer to Australia. And Australia was where she had planned to go next on her world tour of theatre.

Lucy looked at her watch. They were already an hour behind their scheduled departure time and it was getting hot inside the plane. She could feel her thick, wavy, reddish-blonde hair sticking to the back of her neck as a result of the New York heat broiling up from the tarmac. She fiddled with the air vent above her head but nothing happened.

"They won't turn those on till the plane takes off," her neighbor declared. Lucy rolled her eyes and Mr. Tall and Lanky saw this and laughed in agreement. Then he jumped in with, "I'm Malcolm, by the way."

Lucy took his proffered hand and shook it, saying, "I'm Lucy." Then she quickly turned back to her window, hoping to close him out again.

Lucy heard Malcolm stand up and open the overhead luggage bin. A few seconds later she heard the bin slam shut and felt Malcolm plunk down in the seat next to her again.

"Want a chocolate?" she heard him ask.

Lucy turned and saw a big box of good quality chocolates on Malcolm's lap. She grinned. Now she'd talk to him.

~

Joe was picking his way slowly over the raised beds he'd made in his garden, carrying a good handful of irises, and stopping when he saw weeds that needed to be pulled around the young vegetable shoots he'd planted. He looked up when he heard somebody sound a car horn down in front of his house. Must be somebody had pulled in for the shop.

"Woof! Woof! Woof!" barked Maggie, and she loped down the graveled lane from the garden to the house to greet the visitor.

Joe followed, thinking for the umpteenth time that he really ought to build a fence around this garden, to keep the deer out of his vegetables. They'd already been snacking on his bush peas and chard, the two tallest crops this early in the season, and he certainly didn't want them in his tomatoes once they started growing. He let the irises swing at his side as he walked the 150 feet downhill, feet apart, toes turned out, the jaunt in his stride putting bounce in his bushy brown hair. Joe was thirty-three and at 5 foot 10, only average height but he had broad shoulders and well-built upper body muscles from years of wedging clay making him seem more formidable in stature. He had square-jawed good looks and a generous mouth, wore large, dark frame glasses and usually only shaved every third day, leaving just enough stubble on his cheeks and chin to make him look rugged. Not that Joe cared what he looked like; he just cared that he didn't have to take the time to shave every day because his facial hair didn't grow that fast. Today, though, he'd made a point of shaving to honor Lucy's arrival from New York. He cleared his throat noisily and spat on the ground by the cherry tree before coming around the corner of the house.

His visitor, a well-dressed woman of maybe fifty-five or fifty-six, slim with pointy, bird-like features, was standing beside a white Ford Bronco chuckling merrily as she petted his dog.

"Hi," Joe called out.

"Hi there," his visitor replied. "Did you do this?" She was pointing at the two large, white handprints on either side of the dog's belly.

"Yes, indeedy," Joe replied, holding up his right hand as if in evidence. "It's camouflage. So people can't tell us apart."

"Maybe if you'd made them in the shape of hibiscus," the woman teased, eyeing Joe's shirt.

Joe smiled and proudly smoothed one side of his Hawaiian shirt with his free hand. Then he dipped his head, so he could look at his visitor over his glasses with his hazel green eyes. "I got dressed up to go get my girl at the airport," he said, punctuating the "my girl" with a flirtatious lift of his eyebrows.

"Is that who those are for?" the woman asked, nodding at the flowers in Joe's hand.

Joe raised them up when she mentioned them. "Uh huh," he affirmed. "You think I'll get kissed?"

Some of the irises were white with lavender edgings on their petals, some were yellow and the rest were a deep chestnut color that looked almost too rich to be real.

"I think you might," replied the woman.

Joe gazed down at the blossoms that he was cradling in his large hands and could feel the woman watching him. He knew he came across as rough and gruff but that didn't mean he didn't love his flowers. He lifted his eyes and treated her to another of his wide, warm smiles; she blushed. Almost as quickly she snapped her head upright and asked, "Where's your girl coming from?"

"New York."

"How fun. Was she there on vacation?"

"No. She was living there!" Joe made himself sound suitably appalled.

"I take it you're not much of a city boy?"

"Not too much," Joe admitted. "Too many people for my taste. 'Specially in New York. You know what I heard on the radio the other day? I heard some guy describing New York as the second circle of Hell. And it was National Public Radio, so you know it must be true!"

"What was the first?"

"Dallas."

"Oh now," said the woman. "That's not fair. I lived in Dallas once and it wasn't that bad!"

"Were you hot?" Joe asked, baiting her.

"What?" The mischievous look on her face suggested she knew she was being baited but couldn't resist.

"Were you hot in Dallas?" Joe asked again.

"Well sure. Of course I was hot. I mean, it was Dallas."

"Well, there you go. Proves my point!"

"The woman laughed uproariously. Then she stretched her manicured right hand out in his direction. "I'm Marianne, by the way," she volunteered. "Marianne Dunning."

Joe shook her hand, noticing the way the huge, turquoise pendant hanging around her neck picked up the blue of her eyes. "Joe Connors," he replied, then gave her a quizzical look. "Dunning?" he repeated. "Where do I know that name from?"

"You've met my husband."

Joe snapped his fingers and pointed at her, remembering. "The building inspector," he exclaimed.

"Uh huh."

"That son of a gun red tagged me!"

It was an indictment but he said it so good-naturedly that he made Marianne laugh. Joe noticed how the gold tips in her short, loose curls danced in the sunlight as her head bobbed to the rhythm of her laughter.

"You're not supposed to build without a permit," Marianne chided once she'd stopped laughing.

"That's not what I heard. I was talking to this building inspector once – not your husband, some other guy – and he said that none of the upriver people ever got permits. I figured he was giving me permission."

Marianne laughed again. "George told me you had said that." She paused and tipped her head up, gazing at the house Joe had built alongside the highway.

It looked like a gingerbread house with two steep gables pointing sharply towards the sky and a roof of overlapping, brown, cedar shakes. Underneath the roof, the house was made of alternating stretches of vertical logs and cedar shingles with a bay to the right that held the pottery shop. A series of small, mullioned windows circling the bay twinkled light from the inside out and there were identical windows on the second floor that had been arranged in triangles to accent the shape of the gables. The whole thing looked like something out of a fairy tale.

"George likes your house," Marianne told Joe. "I do too."

"Thanks. I wanted to build something that looked like it had always been here. Like it grew out of the ground."

He watched her eyes float over the thick forest on the mountain ridges behind his property and when she brought them back to his house, he could see her appraising the rough-hewn logs, the shakes and shingles abundant with growth ring swirls, the knotty posts holding up the roof over the front porch and the curves in the natural wood railings alongside the front steps.

She looked at him and declared, "You've done that, I'd say. Did you work with an architect?"

"Un uh. I told George – that's your husband, right?" Marianne nodded. "I told George when he asked about drawings that I didn't have any. I just drew it on the hood of my pick-up truck when I figured out what I wanted to build."

"Did the County accept that?"

"Nooooo. They wanted drawings. So I used a brown paper grocery bag from the shop, tore it open so it was one big sheet and drew the plans on the back of that. Then I took them down to the County. The woman behind the counter looked at them, kind of scratching her head – but she accepted them. And then she wanted three hundred some bucks for the permit. I said, "I don't have that kind of money!" but I could tell she was intractable on *that* subject so I said, "But I can make payments…"""

"And she accepted that?"

"She didn't want to. "We don't usually allow people to make payments,"" Joe said, mimicking the County employee. "But I told her it was the only way I could do it. Take it or leave it. So she took it."

His bold, unapologetic manner provoked another burst of laughter from Marianne.

"Hey, people will work with you if you're willing," he added.

"And you were willing?"

"Well, no, not in that case. I would never have bought a building permit if that son of a gun husband of yours hadn't red tagged me. What do I need to give money to some pencil wielding knucklehead in a suit for just so he can tell me what I already know I can do?"

Marianne laughed again. A loud, staccato rumble made them both turn towards the highway, where a log truck was using its Jake brake in the long, shallow descent past Joe's house. The truck was loaded with huge diameter old growth fir logs and both Joe and Marianne watched it go by and sniffed deeply in unison, inhaling the tangy aroma of the fresh cut fir being misted into the air around them.

They grinned at each other, then Joe returned to his narrative. "But five years ago," he said. "I got a speeding ticket, going through Burlington, down below, and I had to go to the Skagit County Courthouse to contest it. The judge reduced it but I still had to pay a hundred dollars – I guess I must have been going fast. Well my girlfriend had taken my pick-up and left me to drive her piece of junk Mustang with the driver's side window that wouldn't roll up and windshield wipers that didn't work and it was raining – hard –

so I had to drive fast!"

"Is this the girlfriend you're going to pick-up at the airport?" Marianne interrupted to ask.

"Oh good Lord, no," replied Joe. "The Mustang lady and I parted company quite some time ago. Anyway," he went on, drawing the word out to change the subject. "I told the judge that I didn't have a hundred dollars, "but I can make you some nice planters for the courthouse," I said. And he said, "Okay." So that's what I did." Joe leaned in towards Marianne and added with obvious pride, "Those planters are still there, right in the courtroom."

"Do they look anything like that one there?" Marianne was pointing at a planter sitting at the base of a big slab of cedar next to the steps to the front porch, on which someone had carved, "Sound Horn."

Joe turned and looked. It was one of his large, round, stoneware planters with mountains drawn on the outside. Mountains in the red slip with an ash glaze over that twinkled in the sunlight. "Probably," he said, twanging the word so hard it lost both letter bs.

"Do you have any more like that?" asked Marianne.

Joe sucked air noisily through his teeth because he really didn't want to say no, even though he knew he had to. "I'm pretty sure I don't," he admitted. Then his face lit up. "But I could make you one."

"That might be an option," Marianne replied, rubbing the point of her chin while still staring at the planter. "Although I need something right now. I have some begonias that need a pot for the summer....." she explained.

"I can never seem to get begonias to make it....." Joe told her.

"They need to be in the shade."

"Is that what it is?"

"Yes. They like it warm but they don't like direct sunlight. So if you can find a shady spot..."

Joe looked to the right of his house, at the area between the cherry tree and his garden. "Maybe under my vine maples...." he mused.

Marianne's face flashed sudden concern. "Am I holding you up from going to the airport?"

"Oh no," Joe replied. "Her plane doesn't get in until 3:30 this afternoon and what time is it now?"

Marianne looked at her watch. "11:15," she told the potter.

"Yeah, I wasn't planning to leave before noon 'cause it takes about two and a half hours to get to the airport from here. Plus Maggie and I always have time for customers. Don't we, Maggie?" The beautiful, clayprinted dog stepped towards her master, pushing her nose into the side of his leg. Maggie was a mix of Chesapeake and Short-Haired Pointer, which showed in the curl to her brown coat along her spine and in her long, slender nose. Joe let his free hand drop down to her ear and scratched it without thinking.

"How long's your girl coming for?" Marianne asked.

"Forever, I hope."

"Oh my. From New York City to here, that's a big change. Do you think she'll be able to take our rain?"

"I would think so," Joe answered. "She's from G.B."

"As in Great Britain?"

"Exactly right. So I doubt the rain will be a problem for her." Then he turned his roguish charm on his visitor and added, "I might though!"

Marianne chuckled. "I bet you might."

Joe looked at the pendant hanging around Marianne's neck again. "Come on," he said, moving towards the front steps of his house. "I'll show you into the shop. Maybe you can give me back some of that money George cost me..."

~

They'd been in the air for a good two hours when Lucy roused herself from a short catnap and peered out the window. She sat up, her curiosity piqued, and pushed her face closer to the window. Down on the ground, underneath them, were huge circles of land that had nothing inside them; no houses, no cars, no industry, no shopping centers. Some of them were dark brown with just the hint of a spiral inside them, others were more of a beige color. They must be agricultural, Lucy thought to herself, although she'd never seen anything like it. It wasn't just their size that impressed her, it was their perfect roundness and the complete lack of anything resembling a human habitation anywhere near them. What it must be, she thought, to have so much land you could create great circles like these that were seemingly isolated. Then she saw four of the circles sitting inside an even bigger square and again, they were devoid of anything suggesting human life in or around them. Except, of course, their very tidiness suggested human interference because the land would never be like that naturally. Some of the circles even had a line in them, going from the outside edge into the center, like a radius. Lucy was agog; she was pretty sure that the whole of England could probably fit inside one of those circles!

She glanced at her neighbor, Malcolm, to ask him what they were but he was fast asleep. She sat back in her seat again, thinking. She'd always been a bit bewildered by how big everything seemed in America compared to England. Like the highway that went past Joe's house; it was what they called a rural and scenic highway but it was spacious and wide, with well-delineated lanes for the two-directional traffic, not the least bit like the narrow, curvy, country roads of England with their tall hedgerows that blocked views so you had to stick to your lane for dear life when driving along them. Even Joe's house, which was pretty small when you didn't include the shop, seemed big to Lucy. Probably because the acreage around it was filled with pasture and trees and mountain ridges, giving the house the impression of being more spacious.

Lucy thought back to August, 1984, the summer she met Joe. He was in the process of building his house and he'd just nailed down the last of the floorboards on the second floor. Or what Lucy called the first floor. "Ground floor, first floor," she explained, pointing at the two levels.

"Nah, nah," Joe rebuffed. "This is America. We call that the second floor."

He'd led her up the ladder to the second floor and asked her to help him lift a hefty cedar log so it could become a post in one of the interior walls. They hoisted the 12 foot log to a stand together and then Joe had her help him guide it down onto a big old nail he had sticking up out of the floor to stop the post from moving once it was in place. It wasn't easy because the log was heavy, and tall, but they got it. "You can come back anytime," Joe commended, tipping his head down so she got a hit of those warm green eyes over his glasses.

And now here she was, two years later, going back to live in that little house. Was it a little house? Or a big house? Lucy thought for a moment. It was a fairytale house, that's what it was, because that's what Joe had made it look like. Lucy had seen shooting stars in the night sky over the second floor that first summer, something she'd never in her life seen before. Shooting stars in a sky that was absolutely laden with tiny twinklings. Big sky. Big land. She looked out the window once more, at the circles down on the ground. Big country, she thought.

~

Joe pointed to the door on the right once they got up to the porch and told Marianne to head on in while he went and wrapped some wet newspaper around the stems of his irises. Then he disappeared through the door in the center of the porch.

The door to the shop, like the one to the house, was single pane glass with cross-grids set in an old wood frame that had been painted lavender and decorated with airbrushed flowers as if someone had been testing a stencil on it. Marianne peeked through one of the small squares of glass as she turned the handle. The pottery was displayed on tables made out of huge, rough-cut rounds of wood sitting on shortened tree trunks that billowed and twisted as they reached down to the floor. The far wall was made of the vertical logs visible from the outside, only they were flat sawn on the interior surface. Running the length of the logs was a slab of rich, dark cedar that Joe was using as a counter to display more of his pottery. To the right of the door was the bay holding five of the small, mullioned windows, and the early afternoon sunlight streamed in through them, lighting the pots on the display tables. It looked like a little gallery built by hobbits in a hollowed out tree trunk, one that was filled with treasures on every surface including the knotholes and root wads.

Marianne lingered on the threshold, as if appreciating the whole before allowing herself to explore the details, then she stepped inside the shop and quietly closed the door behind her. When she turned back around her eyes landed immediately on a first treasure. It was a pitcher, fairly narrow in the base, with a slender, cylindrical form that rose to an even narrower, but decidedly long neck. The whole thing was topped off with a delicate pout of a pouring spout and a wide, comfortable handle ran down one side, from the top of the neck to the middle of the base. Marianne picked it up with her right hand and balanced the bottom on her left, bouncing it gently as if surprised by the lightness of the object. Then she ran her thumb over some tiny flowers that had been carved into the body of the pitcher.

The way their petals folded back on themselves and their stamen hung down exposed in the center suggested that they were alpine tiger lilies, a flower that grew alongside many of the trails in the North Cascades. Marianne smiled as she looked at the pot, then lifted it higher into the air and turned it around slowly, to admire its colors in the sunlight. The flowers were a soft, sky blue, the neck and spout were glazed a charcoal gray, and the rest of the pitcher, from the neck down, was covered in a matte, powdery pink glaze, making the pot, a piece of hard-fired clay, appear almost soft to the touch.

"A little wine to go with your cheese?" Joe asked as he came into the shop sipping some coffee.

Marianne lowered the pot and turned to look at him. "Is that what this is for?" she asked.

"Well, sure. It could be. But then again, it could be for anything you want it to be for once it's yours. Why? Don't you drink wine?"

"Oh yes, I drink wine. But not very often. And I doubt I'd ever decant it. I just think this would look great with some of my lavender in it." Joe watched her raise the pitcher to eye level again. "It would go so well with this pink."

Joe walked over to Marianne, set his coffee mug down on the center table and took the pitcher out of her hands. "I don't know why that glaze does that," he remarked, flipping the pot over to examine it on both sides.

"Does what?"

"Goes pink like that. It's really just a matte white but I changed the formula a couple of firings ago and it's been going that soft pink ever since."

"Well don't change it back," Marianne said, with a sing-song lilt in her voice. "I like it."

"That's what I've been hearing from other customers." Joe placed the pitcher back on the table, lifted up his coffee mug and walked around Marianne to perch on a bar stool he had sitting at the end of the long cedar counter. He propped his feet on one of the cross bars between the legs of the stool, so his knees were at a 90 degree angle to his waist and rested his hands, with the coffee mug between them, in his lap.

Marianne glanced once more at the pitcher on the center table then followed Joe to the counter on the outside wall. Except instead of walking its length to where Joe was sitting, Marianne stopped about mid-way, to examine another pitcher, this one with a ceramic cone coming out of its top. "What's this?" she asked.

"It's a drip coffee pot."

"Is that right?" Marianne sounded fascinated. "Does it make good coffee?"

"*I* think so. Here, I'll get you a cup if you like," and Joe shifted forward on the stool as if he were about to stand up.

"Oh no thanks," Marianne replied quickly, holding her hand up to suggest he need not go any further. "I'll take your word for it." She peered down at the coffee pot. "Does it take longer than the plastic coffee machines?"

"Probably."

"And people don't complain about that?"

"Not to me they don't."

Marianne swung her head from side to side and made a face. "I bet George would."

"You're s'posed to take a long time making coffee," Joe told her. "It's all part of the ritual."

Marianne sighed and crossed in front of Joe to look at the pots on the display table to his right. "George gave up rituals once he started making money."

"County pays that well, huh?"

"No, no, not the County..." Marianne took the lid off a cookie jar and ran her hand softly around the inside edge. "It's his hobby that's paying so well."

Joe had been leaning against the log wall but his excitement at hearing Marianne's words propelled him forward to an upright position, almost spilling his coffee in the process. "Did he finally design that computer program he had in his mind?" Marianne looked at the young potter, her mouth open with surprise. "Hey, George and I spent a long time shooting the shit after we were done with business," Joe told her. "And I had a good time talking to him. It was obvious he was into his computer stuff...."

"Yes, and you told him to go for it if that's what he really wanted to do....."

"I said that?!" Joe went for incredulity just in case he was in trouble here. "Were you not okay with that?"

"No, no." Marianne flapped her free hand around in the air, as if batting away Joe's concerns. "George came back so pumped up after he met you. He loved how you had a dream of building a house with a place in it to sell your pots and how you'd saved materials for it for ten years – isn't that what you told him?"

"Yep. Salvaged whatever I could from the local sawmill and from logging projects and by the time I was ready to start building I had piles everywhere on my 5 acres...."

"George found that inspiring. And he came home and stopped talking about designing a software program and actually did it. And I guess it's a great program because everybody wants it and they're all willing to pay him large amounts of money to get it."

"Well, hot dog! Way to go, George!"

Marianne looked back down at the cookie jar, making a little 'hmm' of doubt in the back of her throat.

"You're not pleased for him?"

"Well sure I am. It's just...." Marianne put the lid back down on the jar and left her hand resting on top of it as she looked at Joe. "These companies don't just want to buy his software program, they want him to work for them too. Which is good because George has now quit his job at the County...."

"Time for me to build an addition!" joked Joe.

Marianne smiled then looked down at the display table again. She opened her mouth as if to say something then changed her mind. She took a step forward and pointed at a shallow, lidded casserole dish, next to the cookie jar. "Can this go in the oven?" she asked.

"Yep. Oven safe, microwave safe and dishwasher safe. So where's George going to work?"

"That's the problem...."

Joe nodded as he sipped his coffee once more; now they were getting somewhere.

".....some of these companies are down in California, in Silicon Valley. And George is flying down there tomorrow, to finalize an offer."

"Oh." Joe paused. "So I guess you're moving to California."

"Maybe."

Joe saw her lips tighten, her eyebrows move together, creating lines of worry above her nose. He dropped his head again, to look at her over his glasses. "I take it you're not much of a California girl?" he said. He'd meant it as a joke but his tone was gentle because he could totally understand her reluctance.

"Not too much," Marianne confessed. She took a big, deep breath, as if plucking up the courage to address this issue, and Joe saw her shoulders relax when she exhaled. "I mean, I'm thrilled that George is finally being successful with his computer stuff but I'm not thrilled about the prospect of leaving Washington."

"How come he doesn't try for a job with that company in Redmond? The one that just went public. I'm always hearing about how well they're doing on the radio."

"They *are* doing well, Very well in fact. But.....I don't know, there's something about California that's luring George right now."

"The paycheck?"

"Could be," she answered, tracing the line of the mountains on the lid of the casserole with her fingers. "Or it could be all that sunshine. George has never had much tolerance for the rain here."

"What rain?"

"Well that's what I say." Marianne took the lid off the casserole to look at the inside. "The trouble is," she continued, "what I say doesn't seem to matter to George all that much these days. And I'm beginning to think that part of the lure in California is my not wanting to go there."

"You think he wants to go without you?" Joe blurted.

Marianne lifted her eyes to meet Joe's and he could see relief in them, as if she were grateful that someone had finally said it. "I think so," she said. "He's been very distant these past few months."

"Maybe he's just freaked out that everyone wants him all of a sudden."

"Could be." She paused, then shrugged. "But even when his mind's not on the computer and I do everything he used to like me to do to make a relaxing moment for us, he can't seem to focus on me. Like I belong in the picture he had of himself in the past but I don't belong in the one he has of himself right now. Or in the future."

"Are you going down to California with him tomorrow?"

She shook her head no. "He didn't invite me." Then she put the lid back on the casserole and flicked her head towards Joe, smiling. "Have you ever taken your girl up Sauk Mountain?"

"Sure," he answered. "She loves to hike. The first date I took her on was a hike into Clear Lake."

"Where's that?"

"The other side of Jackman Ridge." Joe could tell from Marianne's expression that she didn't have a clue what he was talking about so he set down his coffee cup on the slab of cedar and headed for the door again. "Here. I'll show you," he offered.

Marianne trotted behind him as he jogged down the front steps and across the graveled driveway towards a grassy area on one side of his house that was lined with waist-high, Silver fir saplings. Joe stopped and pointed to a blocky ridge south east of his property that was covered in the dark green of alpine conifers. Or almost covered. "That's Jackman," he told Marianne. "And see that clear cut there?" His point drifted slightly to the right, indicating an ugly, bald patch towards the top of the ridge. "If you go up through that clear cut and over the top of the ridge you're supposed to be able to drop down into Clear Lake. But we never found it."

"And I suppose you're going to tell me you ran out of gas," Marianne joked.

"No, no, we really tried. We hiked and hiked and it seemed like all we were doing was going through one clearing after another and never getting to the ridge that we could see right above us. Plus it was hot and at one point I looked back to make sure she was doing okay and saw that her forehead was covered in bugs! So we bagged it. We had a lot of fun though. And I found out she was quite the hiker," he added.

Marianne's face softened and Joe sensed a little poignancy on her part. Here he was at the beginning of his journey of love and she didn't know where she was in hers. He reached out and ran his hand through the needles on one of the Silver firs, encouraging her to do them same with a nod of his head. She did and they both lifted their palms up to their faces and inhaled the piney scent with delight. They grinned at each other again.

"If only life were this uncomplicated," Marianne remarked, letting her hand drop back down to her side again.

Maggie came up to Joe with a stick in her mouth. He stepped forward and threw it for her, in among the vine maples behind his house, as Marianne gazed at Sauk Mountain.

The broad, knuckled top of the mountain was still covered in a good deal of snow but the spring greens were starting to peek through, suggesting the end of the long winter in the high country and the beginning of hiking season.

"How can anyone want to leave all this," Marianne sighed.

"I'm with you there," Joe agreed, bouncing back to her side. "We've got Baker, we've got Shuksan, we've got Sauk. This is some of the most beautiful real estate ever created!"

They stood together in silence, gazing reverentially at the top of the mountain that welcomed people to the upper end of the Skagit River Valley. Sauk wasn't very tall, at 5500 feet, but she looked much more inviting than some of the witches' hat peaks that towered above her further into the Cascades.

"Too bad George isn't here. On a day like today Sauk Mountain's enough to make anyone want to stay," Joe remarked.

"Oh, he's here," Marianne corrected. "I dropped him up at the Cascade River before I came here, so he could go fly-fishing…"

"For Sockeye?" Joe had been thinking about heading up to Bacon Creek to dip his pole in the water for some of his favorite salmon.

"That's what he said," Marianne replied

"Well that's a good sign," Joe suggested. "I mean, if he's fishing for salmon…"

Marianne's cheeks flexed with anger. "I don't know," she said. "I've just got this awful feeling that he's going to go down to California tomorrow and never come back."

"What makes you think that?"

"I couldn't tell you," she replied. "But there was something about the way he announced he wanted to go fly-fishing today…." She paused, then pursed her lips before adding, "Maybe it's just been too long since I've seen his fishing pole!"

Joe smiled as he got an idea. "You know what you need?" he said.

"What?"

"A lovelight!" And he turned away from Marianne and strode back across the driveway.

"A lovelight?" she echoed, following him.

"Come on, I'll show you." And he bounded up to the shop again.

~

Malcolm woke up shortly after Lucy saw the circles on the ground and explained that they were, indeed, crop circles. In Nebraska. Malcolm traveled a lot in the US, he told Lucy, on business. Sales. That's why he was heading out to Seattle. He had a pleasant, resilient manner and the time soon passed with the two of them gabbing about where they'd been and where they were going and why.

"You're moving from Manhattan to the mountains, huh? That's quite the change," Malcolm remarked, flicking his bushy eyebrows up in his forehead.

"Well not really," Lucy amended. "I might spend the summer up in the mountains but I'm going to start looking for work in Seattle as soon as I know my way around a bit and hopefully, I'll find a job and move down there. Then I'll spend my days off in the mountains with my boyfriend."

"What do you do for work?"

"I'm an actress."

"An actress?!" Malcolm was shocked. "An actress from London that's lived in Manhattan and now you're heading to the wilds of Washington to be with some guy. What is he, rich?"

Lucy laughed. "Hardly. He's a potter."

"Oh." Malcolm thought about this. He rubbed the little bit of hair on his chin with his forefinger as he looked up at the overhead vents. Then he looked at Lucy again. "My first wife liked pottery," he told her, "but she didn't like me. She took off one day and I haven't been able to find her since. Took our baby daughter with her. Nine months old. Want to see a picture?"

He was already reaching into his back pocket when he asked and Lucy nodded yes. She was surprised he was sharing this with her but, on the other hand, she was empathetic. Joe also had a daughter that he hadn't seen since she was a few months old and he didn't know where she was either. It was heartbreaking.

"That's her," Malcolm said, tapping on a wallet-sized photo of a plump, smiling baby. "Shelby we called her. She'd be 13 now. And I haven't seen her in all that time. I want to but...." He shrugged. He looked and sounded very matter-of-fact but Lucy was sure it must hurt. Well he probably wouldn't be telling her if it didn't hurt. Then, once again, he bounced on. "These are my other kids," he said, turning to the next photo in his wallet. "Jake and Zachary. And my wife." A smile curled the corners of his mouth as he confided, "She does like me."

Lucy smiled back. "Thank goodness for second chances, eh?"

"Amen to that."

~

Once Joe got inside the shop, he headed back towards the cedar counter and bent down to look through the wooden fruit boxes in which he kept his back stock of pots. Marianne came in behind him and turned to close the door but hesitated when she saw Maggie standing on the porch, looking into the shop with the stick in her mouth. "Can your dog come in," she asked.

"Oh no," said Joe. "She has a tail and tails can be hard on the pots." He turned and peered under the center display table at his dog. "Sit, Maggie," he said. Maggie sat and reluctantly dropped the stick on the porch in front of her.

Marianne closed the door and walked over to where Joe was kneeling on the floor. He swiveled towards her, holding a pot shaped like a hollow gourd on the palm of his hand. The pot had a wide base and a narrow opening at the top, with little heart cutouts all around the body. It was glazed purple and white. "Put a candle down inside this," he told her, sticking his fingers through the opening in the top, "and you'll have George buying you a ticket for the next plane out."

"Is that right?" Marianne reached out delightedly with both hands and gently cupped the object as Joe let go of it.

"I promise you it's true. That's how I got my girl to move out here from New York. With one of these."

"You sent her one?"

"No, I took it when I went and spent a couple of months with her last winter."

Marianne stopped staring at the candle lantern and raised a disbelieving eyebrow in Joe's direction. "I thought you didn't like New York?"

"I don't," Joe admitted. Then he grinned sheepishly. "But I like her."

"I guess you do." Marianne sounded very impressed. She closed one eye and tilted her face slightly away from him. "And you think it's the lovelight that won her heart?"

"I'm pretty sure."

"You don't think it's because you gave up two months of your life to live in a city you detest just to be close to her?"

Joe stood up, waving his head from side to side with sudden shyness. "I don't know," he countered. Then he nudged her with his elbow. "Maybe she just likes my fishing pole."

Marianne laughed, a deep, delighted belly laugh that seemed to release a surfeit of emotions that Joe guessed she'd been holding inside for too long. When she finished, she pointed at the lovelight and announced, "You know, I think you're right. I *do* need one of these."

"You want one with hearts?" Joe asked, crouching down to reach into the box again.

"Well that depends. What else have you got?"

"I've got stars and moons..." and he slid that one up onto the counter above his head, "....and one here with a coyote howling at the moon." Then he glanced around the gallery, to see if there were any others he was missing. "Oo! Oo! Oo!" he exclaimed and rushed over to a window to take a lovelight off the sill. "This one has swans flying over the mountains."

"Swans?"

"Yes. Trumpeter swans. And they always return to the Skagit Valley. So if you light this for George it might give him the idea that this is where he needs to come back to. Like the swans."

Marianne crossed the room and carefully took the candle lantern out of Joe's hands. She held it up to the light and turned it around, examining every inch of it. "Do you think I'll get kissed?" she asked with a glint in her eye.

"Guaranteed!" Joe declared.

And they grinned at each other for a third time.

~

Lucy felt her stomach lurch just as the seatbelt light pinged on above her head. "I guess we've started our descent," Malcolm remarked, stuffing some magazines he'd been reading into his briefcase before pushing it back under his seat. Lucy also began the process of stowing her personal items and she buckled her seat belt at the same time as Malcolm buckled his. He glanced at his watch. "Three hours behind schedule. I guess we didn't make up any time after that delay in New York," He shrugged. "Oh well. Doesn't matter to me. I was just going to head to a hotel and get ready for tomorrow anyway. Call my family. What about you? Will your guy have waited, do you think?"

Lucy lifted her shoulders and eyebrows. "I think so," she said.

But she offered just enough of a smile to suggest she knew so. "After all, he waited two years for me to join him," she added. "I think he'll wait the extra few hours."

Malcolm grinned at her. "That's the spirit," he declared.

~

Marianne and Joe walked out of the shop and back towards the Bronco together, Marianne clutching a brown bag containing the lovelight and the narrow-necked pitcher from the center table.

"You tell George to leave some of those Sockeye for me," Joe teased.

"Will do," Marianne replied. "And good luck with your girl. What's her name, by the way?"

"Lucy."

"Is she a potter too?"

"No, she's an actress."

"An actress?!" Marianne stopped. She looked first to the right, then to the left, her mouth wide open. "She's leaving the lights and glamour and hype of Broadway to come out and live in the middle of *nowhere*?! I mean, it's beautiful up here but it's very rural. And pretty sleepy."

"Hey, I offered to build her a theatre," Joe said, feeling himself getting defensive. He paused and tried lightening the tone again. "And now that George has stopped working for the County...."

Marianne stared at him with her turquoise blue eyes and Joe wondered if she were trying to determine his value compared to the value of a career on Broadway.

"You don't think I'm worth it?" he asked softly.

"No, no, I would never say that," countered Marianne. "I'm sure your girlfriend finds you and your little pottery shop very charming. But....." She hesitated, and looked to her left again.

Joe followed her gaze out to the wide expanse of pasture next to his house and he knew that all around him, beyond what either of them could see, was just more pasture leading into woods that turned into thick forests that climbed the mountain ridges. The only thing that cut through this abundant greenery was the highway and that could be pretty sleepy at times too.

"....for someone whose art form requires being in the city,"

Marianne continued, "living up here would mean she's got her work cut out for her."

"Don't I know it," Joe agreed. He opened the door of the Bronco and held it open while Marianne climbed into the driver's seat. "And you can be sure if there's anyone that can make things more complicated than they need to be," he said, pointing his thumb back towards his chest, "it's me!"

Marianne chuckled. She placed her bag of pottery on the empty passenger seat and started the engine. "I bet you'll be a great help," she reassured him. She buckled herself in, wrinkling her nose as she peered up at the sky through the open door. "They said it was going to rain later."

"Yeah." Joe turned slightly and also looked up at the sky. It was the kind of clear, dazzling blue that made him want to stand at the edge of a high mountain lake and fish. "You couldn't tell it by that sky but I'd better go cover my slow clay. Just in case."

"Slow clay?"

"Well that's what I call it. I make clay outside and let it dry sloooooowly, under the sun." He closed the door for Marianne and waved as she took her foot of the brake, and let the Bronco drift backwards, down the driveway.

Then he paused and looked up at the sky again as he heard a plane passing overhead. Marianne's obvious concern about Lucy's living here had definitely got to him. Sometimes he wondered if his first marriage would have lasted if he and his wife had bought acreage closer to a city. Not that Lucy had agreed to marry him. No, he hadn't got her to bite on that lure yet. But Joe was persistent when he wanted something and he'd been hoping that Lucy would take the lure once she tried life out here for real. But what if he were wrong? The Upper Skagit was beautiful but it was a tough place to make a living. And these mountains were filled with the memories of many who had tried and failed. Was he taking Lucy away from everything that felt familiar or welcoming her to the adventure of a lifetime? He reflected on this as he walked back up to his clay and slid a piece of sheet metal over it. Who knew? He looked down at his dog. "We like it here, don't we, Maggie?"

The beautiful brown dog thumped her tail on the ground behind her. "Woof!" she replied.

23884962R00052

Made in the USA
Columbia, SC
18 August 2018